Tales of the Shonri:
City of Lights

Stephen Godden

FIREDANCE BOOKS

First published in the UK by Firedance Books in 2012.

Copyright © 2011 Stephen Godden.

Cover illustration and design copyright © 2012 Gary Bonn and William Sauer.

ISBN: 978-1-909256-14-9

Firedance Books

firedancebooks.com

Dedication

To my Mam and Da. I'm sorry I took too long.

CHAPTER ONE

MEDINA KNEW HE WOULD BE LEAVING her soon, now that she had healed his wounds. She could see it in the impatient movement of his hands upon the bed-covers, in his almond eyes filled with shaded light, and in his mouth, a tight line of grief across his face.

Soldat, one of the Seven Shonri, the last of the originals.

His skin dark against the white cotton of the sheets. His gaze, restless and cold, darting around the small room. His mind open to her, seeking escape from the guilt to come, but finding no sanctuary.

Careful now, she had to be careful.

'Where's my armour?' he asked, in brutal tones to disguise the anguish behind his face.

'Clean and patched,' she answered, in soft tones to keep him there a little while longer.

He itched to return to the fight, to return to the slow stuttering war against those who had destroyed the world in the pursuit of their greed. Battles fought in the dark places, in the hidden places, in a war of the hunters and the hunted—with the roles always in doubt.

'My weapons?'

'Sharpened and oiled.'

'I need them.' The silver lines of electrum within Soldat's skin flared bright in the darkened room; Scryer-marks, lines that coiled around every muscle, every sinew, every nerve and blood vessel, both a gift and a curse. A protection against the magic of his enemies and a remembrance of all he had lost.

Soldat had taken that gift, that curse, and led the revolt against Basilard, the Mage who cursed them with the marks of the Shonri, who made them into his magic-cast soldiers, who thought himself their master. Basilard had died for that mistake and so the war began.

The war against the Magi.

Careful now, the rage she stoked could overwhelm her. He was so very powerful.

Medina traced a glimmering line of silver from his brow to his neck. The soothing touch of her hand gentled him. 'I only seek a proper farewell,' she whispered into his ear.

He shifted under her touch. 'I am Shonri, one of the Seven,' he said. 'I could break you in two with these hands.' He showed her the scars across his palms, scars etched into his skin by the sharp edges of his enemies' bones shattering under his grasp. Medina made certain when he lifted those mighty hands his fingers brushed against her breast; her hard nipple against his tough skin, with only the thinnest layer of soft cotton between the two. A furious desire tore through him.

She was so very beautiful.

Medina smiled at the thought purloined and whispered, 'I'm strong.' Her lips brushed his ear, bolstering the connection, closing out the other, riding upon his desire, until she touched his all too human soul. 'A healer. Whatever harm you do I can repair.'

'I—'

'Be gentle with me.'

There was no gainsaying this raging desire, no stopping his hands when they ripped open her chemise. His mouth quested, found the hard erect bud of her nipple. She tasted of wild flowers and he sucked her deep into his mouth, biting the aureole, before dragging his teeth back to tip.

She gasped and threw back her head, her eyes exultant as she pulled his head forward, tighter against her, holding him there as he sucked and licked and bit. His tongue, his teeth, his lips, ranged over her body. He tore her skirt away as if it were made of paper, snapped her undergarments, flung them across the room.

No need to be careful now, he was hers for the taking.

Her legs trembled when she pulled back the sheets and thrust herself upon him. His hands slid down to cup her buttocks, pulling her open, driving himself deeper into her, controlling her movements, his penetration. She weighed so little in his enhanced arms. He kept control, kept his grip from tearing open her flesh.

She needed him to lose control and moved above him, pulling upon the thread between his soul and hers. The tension in his arms, in his hands, in his body; the tension she needed to release.

He pushed against her, the pressure rising, rising, pulsing within him, higher, harder, the light shining, flaring, building.

Her head tipped back, her cries frantic, her eyes now shut tight against the raging power filling this tiny room. His powerful shoulders tensed beneath her hands. The heat in his Scryer-marks poured into her. This was what she wanted, needed; this was why she had come to this rude shack on the edge of the wilderness. Close now, closer still, his cries matching hers, his breath upon her skin.

Timing is everything.

Lost now in the wonderful sensation of her long hair on his face, Soldat revelled in her scent. It had been so long, so very, very long. He had forgotten what this felt like. The Magi had taken so much from him. He thrust and gasped and pulled her tight. His fingers slippery with her blood, but he didn't care, the moment of release coming... coming...

She pulled away from him, letting his seed spill across the sanctified cotton of the sheets. Her wounds, torn open by his mighty hands, slowly closed and healed without any fuss.

'Did I hurt you?' he asked, guilt in his golden eyes.

'It doesn't matter.' She leaned down and kissed him.

'I—'

'It doesn't matter,' she repeated, hushing him.

He slid out of the bed into the silence that filled the room now the magic had passed. He found his clothes, his armour and his weapons in the outer room. A pause, as he lifted the locket that contained locks of hair from his wife and children. His dead wife, his dead children, the metal cold against his skin when he lifted the chain over his head. He dressed quickly, shame burning against his heart.

Dressed in a robe of silken splendour, without a word, she waved him on his way.

Soldat returned to the fight, her taste upon his lips.

Medina watched him striding into the cool air of a spring evening and sighed deeply. 'My beautiful, sweet, Soldat.' She pulled the silk tighter around her body, watching him until he disappeared into the twilight.

She returned to the bed, working quickly, scraping up his spilled seed from the sheets, adding it to the vial with the other bodily fluids she collected while he lay injured, along with a lock of his hair, the clippings from his nails, and a single drop of Scryer electrum retrieved, with great care, while he lay comatose that first night. She shook the vial and the liquid inside turned crow-black.

Medina smiled softly and added the vial to the other six in the strongbox beneath her bed.

CHAPTER TWO

SPRING TURNED INTO SUMMER AND, far away from Medina's shack on the edge of the wilderness, other Shonri waited in air heavy as syrup, dense with magic, treacle thick.

Wildflowers cascaded down the side of the valley, birds sang in the trees as they built their nests, the sharp, spiked flavour of pinesap in the air. Haram, another of the Seven, moved quietly through the forest and kept his mind hushed. So much magic here; a dangerous place for an ambush, but the Lamia Cinome rarely left the safety of these mountains. He checked his weapons, his harness, and looked across the valley at his sacrificial lambs.

The first real mission for those newborn Shonri, their training over, their time as hunters begun. He wondered how many would survive their first contact, especially against such a dangerous enemy.

'They'll be fine.' Felice, the Conduit of the Seven, sent the thought into his mind. 'You've trained them well.'

'This isn't training, Felice.' Haram sent the reply. 'Hush now, she comes.'

His Scryer-marks muted under the trees. He hoped the newborns could keep theirs under control, keep their minds hushed and stay hidden. They were trained, they were transformed, the Machine had accepted their sacrifice—but they were new to this war, to the ways of the Lamias, the mind-rapers.

If the newborns survived this combat then they became free to wander alone, to hunt alone. They would have passed their last test.

Across the valley, the newborn Shonri Anria licked her lips. This was it, the moment she had fought towards through all the training, the deprivation. She endured the pain and the humiliation, tolerated the misery and the exhaustion, accepted the terror of the Machine's touch and all that touch involved. The Scryer-marks within her thin, new, as she was new, but the power, the strength, the speed they granted filled her with savage joy. She had to control that joy, keep her mind hushed—they hunted a Lamia this day.

They hunted Cinome.

Five other young Shonri ranged along the cliff-top beside her. Their crossbows loaded with simple folded-steel bolts, which pierced armour but were not as dangerous as Haram's experimental weapons. Would they be enough?

Anria had been a music student in the City of Lights. A favoured child of the city, raised in wealth and splendour, because her father pandered to the whims of the Magi. Until his fall from grace threw his family into the brutal underbelly of that city. Her eyes opened to the truth of her world and Anria had sought out the Shonri, sought out redemption for all she had done in ignorant security.

Korat lay close beside her. 'She thinks she's safe here,' he whispered, his finger tight on the trigger of his crossbow. 'She thinks she's safe.'

Perhaps, Anria thought, but the mind-raper had every reason to think herself safe, this was her land, her mountain, her sanctuary; but a new dead zone grew to the west. A place where the magic became thin, dissipated, died and took away her power. Cinome didn't know about that. Haram had discovered it, discovered what caused it, formed new alliances for the war, laid his plans, and brought the newborns here to fight their first true battle.

'Quiet, Korat,' Anria murmured. 'She will sense your presence.'

'Don't tell me what to do.' Korat sneered at her over the top of his crossbow. 'Scared, poor little rich girl?'

Anria dropped her gaze. Korat had been a slave once. Anria had once owned slaves.

Across the valley, from his hiding place, Haram surveyed the enemy column. Damn, this would be harder than expected.

In the distance, Cinome rode upon a carriage pulled by six Turmerix. Long segmented bodies with six legs, mandible jaws clicking and clacking, their stubby antennae moving slowly, placidly, around their heads. Haram could weep to see them in such a state, but he had other things to think about besides tempered Turmerix slaves.

Three Callort fighting pairs plodded along in the vanguard of the procession, huge, hulking creatures whose stony skin resisted the sharpest of normal blades, with heavy clubs resting upon their shoulders. Haram had expected, had planned for, two pairs but not three. Have to be accurate then. He checked back along the line.

Courtiers, humans and others, traitors to everything decent in the world, clustered alongside the mind-raper's carriage. Killing them would be a pleasure. He had ordered the newborns to fire upon them, to sow confusion, to give Haram time to strike.

An acceptable risk. Three pairs of Callorts made things difficult, but not impossible. A minor setback, not enough to abort the attack.

A flash of white near the end of the line. Haram closed his eyes for a moment, cursed softly, and then opened them again. A talon of Inoxit, twelve of the creatures, bone-white exoskeletons glimmering, they flowed over the ground on six of their eight legs, while the other two limbs held weapons in claws adapted into hands. Their compound eyes glittered in the dappled sunlight beneath the trees. A talon of Inoxit, too many of the fast little buggers for his untried newborns, and he couldn't defend them, not this day. Not while he attacked such as Cinome.

Another day then.

Haram raised his hand to call off the ambush.

Too late.

Anria saw Korat's Scryer-marks flare even as she spotted the talon of Inoxit at the end of the enemy column. His hatred too bold, too strong, he couldn't hold it in when he saw Cinome again, the mind-raper who once owned him.

It all became clear now. His harsh words when drunk, his excitement at this mission. He'd never used her name. Always he'd called the creature the mind-raper. Never Cinome, never Lamia, and now his hatred would kill them all.

His Scryer-marks flared so bright.

Haram snarled into the air. One of the newborns had become overeager, had let their mind become too loud.

The Inoxit turned as one body, rushed up the slope of the narrow valley towards where the newborn Shonri lay hidden. Even the sheer cliff offered no resistance to the creatures; they skittered upwards, flowing over the rock, so very fast.

Haram lifted the heavy crossbow, lined up a bolt on one of the Callorts. He had to try to draw the Inoxit away from the newborns. He had expected some to die in this battle, but the Inoxit would slaughter them all. A faint pressure on the trigger of the crossbow and the bolt flew true to thud into a Callort chest. The diamond-clay splattered, spread, exploded, and drove shards of diamond into the Callort's body through its rocklike skin, scything through its internal organs. Thick black blood erupted from the Callort's mouth and nose. It crumpled to the ground.

Haram heard the battle cries and screams of the newborn Shonri as they started to die.

'Work faster. Work faster,' Felice sent. *'I cannot hold her forever. I am too far away and she is Cinome.'*

'Quiet,' he snapped into the mind connection, hooked the string into the goat-head claw attached to his belt, stuck his foot through the stirrup at the front of the crossbow, and straightened his back, using the strength of a Shonri to draw back the steel arms. A click as the trigger mechanism grabbed hold of the string. Another bolt, a heavier bolt, slotted into place. Ready. He lifted the crossbow.

Callorts are faster than they look. Three rushed upwards towards his position. The last two stayed down beside the carriage, protecting their mistress.

Haram squeezed the trigger.

The bolt struck the ground in front of the attacking Callorts and exploded, splashed diamond-clay over two of the creatures, a ripple of reports as the clay ignited. Two Callorts crumpled.

But one did not.

Haram dropped the crossbow, took three steps, and launched himself into the air.

CHAPTER THREE

'YOU HAVE NEED OF WHAT?' Medina asked Calderan, who came hot and loose from yet another lost battle. His face battered and bruised by Shonri fists but he survived. Calderan had a talent for survival, a talent for escape, for leaving others to die in his stead. He kept a cold and imperious expression upon that brutalised face, but Medina could feel the waves of heat beneath his skin. Fire-magi were so very dangerous.

This made them so much fun to play with.

'They hide,' Calderan rasped through a throat ruined by too many hours chanting above braziers to hone his control of the flames. 'They make more, more Shonri, an army of them.'

'Not quite an army, Calderan. They are a little too specialised for that.' Medina smiled at the irritation the Fire-mage hid behind his bruises; he could not hide his emotions from her.

'They make more. That requires a place, a location, a hidden area where we cannot go.'

'A dead zone.'

'No, Witch.' Calderan itched to strike Medina down, a flame of anger eating away at his restraint. She had offered to heal him for the price of his seed, then changed her mind with a sniff when he was naked, saying, 'I do have standards, you know'.

The look on his face had been a delight.

He tried to mollify his tone, to use guile, but this was not his strongest suit. 'A dead zone wouldn't allow the transformation, wouldn't allow the Machine to work its magic. The Scryer-marks wouldn't flow. They need a place where the magic runs hot and slow to make more Shonri. We need to know where that place is.'

'Ah I see, my wizened old wizard, you need to see their paths upon the world.'

'I do. We do. The Twelve will pay well for this.'

The Twelve, the council of Magi, ruled the world with malice and brutality. Vicious, uninhibited civil wars between Magi still broke out from time to time, mostly over who sat in the seats of the Twelve, but the council itself always endured and the Mage Wars had not returned.

Medina considered the request. To give the Magi a weapon against the Shonri: should she do this? A mental shrug. Why not?

'Very well, Calderan, I can do this thing. Leave me now and I will perform the rites. You will receive your answer in due course.' She did so like to use bureaucratic language against one of the Twelve; a slight refrain upon their interminable edicts.

'I want to know now,' Calderan said. He leaned forward, flames behind his eyes.

'And after I have gifted you such knowledge, what further need have you of me? It's obvious your man-root has seen better days, so the joys of the flesh are beyond you.' A little bit more of his self-esteem cut away. Snick. 'You don't require healing of anything more than the surface of your poor, battered, unhandsome visage,' snick, 'and that only requires time to heal. So why should you not kill me once the deed is done and the pathways sketched?'

'You are Medina, none would harm you.'

'You are Calderan, none would trust you.' Snick. Medina grew tired of the game. 'Leave now. Go about your business. I shall send word when I have the item you require.'

'That is not acceptable.'

'That is what it is.'

Calderan's fists clenched tight as he held back the anger. The stench of sulphur billowed from his overheated head. He so wished to kill her now, to strike her down, to burn her to a crisp, his magic wild with the need.

Had she pushed too hard?

'Very well, Witch, it shall be as you say.'

Obviously not. Time to dance at the volcano's edge once more. Such fun to be had with one such as Calderan. 'Good.' She clicked her fingers together. 'Payment in advance.'

'You—'

'Don't trust you, my dear battered Mage, remember?'

His eyes seethed, showing the inferno of his mind.

'Oh and Calderan, don't look for me here once this is over. Because I'll be gone upon the wings of an eagle.'

Chapter Four

HARAM DIVED OVER THE ONRUSHING CALLORT and somersaulted through the air in a tight tuck, landing behind the dumb creature. He rolled once, twice, and came to a halt on his knees, raised his arms, triggered the spring bows strapped to his forearms.

The Callort fighting pair guarding Cinome staggered backwards as the diamond-clay bolts exploded. They crumpled, fell, black blood spilled across the dirt.

Haram didn't stop to deal with the Callort behind him. With a shrug of the shoulder and a twist of the wrist, he pulled his battleaxe from the holster on his back. Double blades atop a shaft of solid steel, none but a Shonri could hope to wield such a heavy weapon; in his hands it swept through the air with speed and precision. He drove forward into the mass of sycophants.

They threw themselves at him, not just the soldiers, but the courtiers too. Unarmed men and women in fine clothes attacking him with berserker savagery.

'She forces a compulsion into their mind,' Felice informed. *'She's almost free. I can't hold her much longer.'*

Haram didn't reply. He couldn't afford the lapse in concentration. His axe whirled around him, spinning, swirling, cutting through the courtiers and soldiers like a scythe through weeds. They barely slowed him, but he knew they were not expected to win.

The last Callort, enraged, smashed his way towards Haram through the courtiers in its path. A rain of blood and brains spattered on the ground.

On the ridge above Haram's battle, Anria fought her own. She stabbed at the Inoxit in front of her with her left-hand blade while she parried the blow of the Inoxit beside her with her right. She only just managed the

13

parry. Too slow. She'd chosen twin longswords to be like Terin, the Fast One, the Shonri who fought with a brace of force blades and cut swathes through any that stood before her. But Anria wasn't Terin; she didn't have her speed, her balance, her fierce attacking instincts.

Ego led Anria to make a mistake in choosing her weapons.

And Korat died for it.

Anria was fast and agile, but two blades don't make a good defence against creatures as quick as the Inoxit or as difficult to kill. Sheer off a leg and they kept on coming. Sheer off half the face and they kept on fighting. Ferocious, implacable death in a white-boned body barely four feet tall.

Korat threw himself upon an Inoxit spear aimed at Anria's back. His shield smashed in the Inoxit's face. His blade stabbed its gut. He killed his killer, but died because Anria was too slow to defend herself properly.

Another sequence of parries and counter-strikes. Anria tried to move back, diagonally to her left, away from the attacking Inoxit, but she was running out of room. The cliff-edge hemmed her in. She could hear the cries and screams of her comrades as they fought their own battles on the ridgeline.

How many Inoxit remained? She could not spare the time to look up, to see, to judge the chances of victory, though she would, by then, be dead.

Just when they had her, the Inoxit stopped. Anria threw a fast lunge, but one of the creatures slapped her blade away. En masse, the remaining Inoxit scuttled away down the hill.

Anria sagged to her knees, her breath coming in deep gasps, sweat beaded across her face. She surveyed the battlefield. Three Inoxit bodies, their carapaces smashed in, lay scattered across the top of the cliff.

And three young Shonri, on their first real hunt, lay dead amongst the wreckage. They had not won a victory here. Death had called for them and then, for some reason, the Inoxit scuttled away and left them alive.

Anria staggered over to Korat's body. She closed his staring eyes and stood for a moment, gazing upon the corpse of this man who had disdained her with all his might and yet, when needed, had stepped in front of a blade aimed at her back. She owed him her life. A comrade falls and you pay homage to them.

She sneered at the longswords in her hands. Such a fool she'd been. She wasn't Terin.

The longswords clattered onto the rock. Anria picked up Korat's shield, Korat's double-edged broadsword. The shield weighed heavy on her left arm and the sword had a different balance to her old blades, but she'd adjust.

Today, she became Shonri.

To her right, Timon tied a bandage around his torn arm. 'Now what?' he asked.

'Now we follow the plan,' Anria replied. She slid her new sword into her belt and gripped Jasmin's shoulder. 'Can you walk?'

Jasmin, her scalp ripped open, blood flowing down her face, said, 'Bandage this up and I can run.'

Beside Cinome's carriage, Haram shifted his battle-axe to a one-handed grip as the last Callort charged. He lifted the axe, accepting the strike of the Callort's club. The force of the blow staggered him, but he stepped in, slapped a disc of diamond-clay onto the creature's chest, smiled, and threw himself backwards.

The Callort stopped, looked stupidly down at the disc of clay, tried to brush it away with one stubby finger. The clay exploded and the last Callort crumpled.

'She's almost free,' Felice warned. *'She's called out to the Inoxit. They come.'*

Haram killed the last few courtiers in his way, clambered up into the carriage and grabbed Cinome with one strong hand. His Scryer-marks nullified her magic.

She spat at him. 'Shonri slug.'

Haram wiped the spittle from his face and punched her unconscious, taking great care not to crush her skull. She couldn't die here.

He threw her comatose form over his shoulder and dropped a clay jar into the middle of the team of Turmerix that pulled the carriage. Tempered Turmerix think only of food and sex. They had already begun to eat the dead bodies around them.

The weight of the mind-raper on his shoulder hardly bothered Haram. Her present body was slight, petite, with golden, waist-length hair that trailed in the gore upon the road as Haram sprinted toward a stream. With the Lamia unconscious, the Inoxit would be forced to follow by scent now; there was no other way to track Cinome while he maintained a grip on her. His Scryer-marks blazed where his flesh touched hers, stifling her magic, but the strain told against his strength. So much force, so much energy required to hold a Lamia tight within her stolen body, and this was Cinome: the Lamia of the Twelve.

He could kill these Inoxit with ease, his weapons and skills stronger than those of the newborns, but if he released this Lamia, even for an instant, she'd flee this body.

Not even Felice could help him now, not through the blaze of his Scryer-marks as they negated the Lamia's powerful magic.

Behind him, the Inoxit swarmed over the carriage, scenting, tasting, trying to find his trail.

One of the Turmerix carriage beasts tried to eat the clay jar.

The explosion ripped through the six Turmerix. Their bones became missiles. Shrapnel smashed through the Inoxit, killing three more of the creatures.

Haram grinned as he leapt down into the stream. It is always good to release slaves tempered into a bland hell, and if you can kill a few of the enemy at the same time, then it's doubly sweet.

CHAPTER FIVE

'THIS WORLD IS BROKEN,' SOLDAT said into the warm air. He knelt upon the grass, the scent of Medina still lying on his skin. Months had passed, days lengthened, summer came, and still her scent lay upon him. And the shame.

He closed his eyes. His breathing slowed, almost stopped. His heart rate deliberate, quiet. The rushing sound of blood in his ears unheeded. His spirit soared free and looked upon the world the Magi had created.

Mountains reared next to shattered spots where their sisters had tumbled into mighty gorges. Ocean currents swept around bubbling cauldrons of magical energy still seething on the seabed. Whole continents denuded of all higher life forms, darkened, burned clean, with only bacteria regaining a tenuous foothold upon their devastated landscapes.

Only one continent remained green and troubled in this sprawling catastrophe of a world.

Just one.

Above it, the magic still flowed in streams of energy. Streams that, invisible to the untalented, reared up over the dead zones like wind whipping over mountaintops.

In those streams of magic flew the Manta-ships, huge ungainly creatures, force-grown by enchantments. Their jet-black bodies swam through the currents of magic flowing above the land. The darkness of their auras told of their dreams: dreams of diving, of splashing into the sea, of shrugging off the cabins welded to their backs, of turning, of devouring their tormentors, of being free once more.

Beneath the land, below the Mantas, Worm-trains slithered through slime-slicked tunnels. Their tendrils sensing their way, their auras cast before them, tempted by the dead zones to turn, to smash through the rock, to find a new path, to undulate, to rasp off the crystal chambers embedded in their flesh, to grind their tormentors to paste, to ride up and over them, and to be free once more.

Soldat smiled at the thought that some Mantas, some Worms, managed these feats of rebellion. But most didn't, the magic wound too tight around them, the noose too sharp to cast off.

To the south lay desert, so hot, so dry, that it would kill an unprepared human in hours, not days. To the north lay sheets of ice, so cold, so bitter, that it would kill an unprepared human in minutes, not hours. To the east, mighty rivers fed by melting ice flowed into the sea, drowning cities and farmlands. To the west, a great mountain range bisected the sky, broken peaks like rotten teeth biting against God.

Nevertheless, there was life here.

Forested carpets of green, lakes like sapphires, farms, towns, cities where humans bustled but kept their eyes shut, their mouths closed, and lived upon the sufferance of the Magi.

Soldat knelt in the foothills of a smaller mountain range, cast upon the earth like a rumpled blanket thrown across a floor. He opened his eyes, lifted his burden once more, and walked into the small valley—a green valley, a place of peace in a world deafened by the cries of those that perished.

Nobody lived here anymore. Birds sang in the small woodland by the river, rabbits scuttled between the overgrown trees, goats grazed, eagles hunted, but no human lived here.

Soldat drew his cloak about him as he entered the valley. Strode across the potholed surface of a road fast succumbing to cold winters and hot summers. He knew this place. He stopped often to gaze at some scene, upon some place he had known as a child. Only one intimately acquainted with this landscape would look upon it now with such despair.

Onward he walked with his smooth gait, to the ruins of the town beside the fallen bridge. He strode up the main street, passing houses, shops, a library, a pub, and the old church: gaping, roofless, toothless monuments to all that he had lost.

The church had lost its steeple but the old yew tree still grew in its grounds. Soldat studied it for a moment; some of the branches needed trimming before the summer heat made such work unwise. The flexible saw at his belt cut through wood as easily as it did the necks of Magi who cracked the world.

He wiped the moss from his hand after vaulting over the remains of the wall. He hadn't needed to jump the wall, he could have found a gap easily enough, but he had vaulted it many times as a boy and the memory made him smile.

Jani had loved him for that, for his strength, for his dexterity, for his agility, and for his smile. She had loved him, he had loved her, and they had wed. In the world now gone, he'd cared for the churchyard and run the local pub. She'd arranged flowers in the church and run the local library. Good books and good ale, what more could a good town possibly need?

They raised their children to be honest, decent, kind, never to raise a hand in anger, always to seek the other way, the quiet way, the way of words not blows.

Until the Magi came.

Soldat stood before the graves of his wife, his children, his town. So many graves. Most held skeletons he'd found within the smashed houses after he returned from the rebellion. Some were older than that. He'd buried his wife and then his children after the plague struck. Some mistaken attack launched by a Mage lord whom Soldat had never considered important—until he took away Soldat's family.

'Spring again, Jani.' Soldat spoke to the headstone of his wife's grave. 'Just came back to tidy things up a bit.' He pulled the razor-sharp scythes from his belt. With strokes as delicate as when he severed the throat of a Mage, he cleared away the weeds and the grass around the rose bush he had planted years before. Jani had always loved roses.

'I killed more of them, Jani,' he said softly, remembering with every stroke of the blades. 'Still more left, but I'll finish the job.'

He paused and laid his hand upon the stone.

'I'll finish the job.'

CHAPTER SIX

ANRIA CHANGED THE DRESSING on Jasmin's head, which had come loose during their frenzied dash to the rendezvous point. With Timon by their side, they clambered down the side of a waterfall and then rested within its cool spray, waiting for Haram. The river, a cascade of foam and noise, roared away down the valley, but their senses were keener than human and they heard Haram's footsteps above the falls.

Haram barely paused, skipping down the rocks with nary a misplaced step.

Anria squinted, letting her Scryer-marks increase the power of her sight. She grinned at Timon and Jasmin. 'He has her.'

'It's not over yet,' Timon said as Haram approached.

'The others?' Haram asked Anria. Only three of the six newborn Shonri at the rendezvous point beyond the falls and only Anria unwounded. No surprise, he'd always known she was the best of his trainees, even if she didn't know it herself.

She shook her head. 'Too many Inoxit, we didn't stand a chance.'

Haram noted the shield on her arm and the sword pushed through her belt: Korat's weapons. So what had the boy done to deserve that honour? Korat had baited Anria at every opportunity. Haram had been surprised when the Machine accepted his sacrifice.

'Why the Inoxit?' Timon asked, pale from blood loss. His Scryer-marks pulsed slow lines of silver as they tried to heal the wound. Too much damage; he'd lose that arm if they didn't get him to a healer soon. Which was, of course, impossible.

'Inoxit are not just guards,' Anria said.

'Shonri hunters,' Timon said. 'I know.'

'More than that.' Anria settled her sword on her belt. 'This wasn't a hunt. We were not expected.'

'Couriers.' Jasmin swayed on her feet.

'They carry a spell?' Timon looked at Haram.

'Most likely.' Haram dumped Cinome from his shoulder onto the ground without releasing his grip upon her flesh. He knew she was awake, because she'd pissed on his shoulder not five minutes ago, leaving a trail for the Inoxit. 'Why the Inoxit, mind-raper? What do they carry?'

'The futility of trusting spies.' Cinome's high-pitched voice was harsh on the ears, the voice of a petulant brat.

Haram slapped her with his free hand.

'You can do nothing to me, slug,' Cinome said. 'Destroy this body if you wish, I will simply find a new one. Not even your precious Felice can hold me in a corpse. So kill me, Haram the Crafty, and release me from the stench of your presence.'

'Nice that you know my name, you mind-raping bitch.'

'Will the Inoxit follow?' Anria asked.

'Oh the baby slug is so scared, so sad.' Cinome put on a sad face.

'Can we reach the mine?' Anria looked up the slope.

'The mine,' Cinome said. 'Oh… you think that darkness will aid you against my little beauties.'

Haram slapped her unconscious again and snapped at Anria, 'Don't give the bitch any more information than you have to.'

'Sorry.'

'No matter, what's done is done, just remember in future. She ain't dead yet. If she escapes and finds her way to the Turmerix hive…' Haram scratched at his face. A talon of Inoxit was a single interlinked mind and with half its components dead, this mind had lost a great deal of its cohesion. 'She'll have to die now. We killed enough of the Inoxit talon to diminish their ability to think. Their orders will conflict, protect this bitch or transport the spell. They'll revert to whichever command is strongest.'

'So either they transport the spell to its destination and we live, or they chase us to protect the mind-raper and we die,' Timon said.

'Aye.' Haram remembered the frenzied attack of the unarmed couriers. 'They'll chase.'

'You're sure?'

'This bitch's last orders were to kill us.' Haram shook the unconscious Cinome and threw her back over his shoulder. 'She'd have driven those orders rather deep and painted them rather bold. The Inoxit'll chase.'

'Can we reach the mine?' Anria asked again.

'It'll be difficult.' Haram glanced at the wounded Timon and Jasmin. 'Once we leave the river they'll find our scent again. They'll hunt us across the moorland.'

'I'll stay,' Timon said.

'As will I,' said Jasmin.

Haram nodded; he'd expected nothing less. 'Try to stay alive.'

'Unlikely,' Timon replied.

Haram hefted a clay jar. 'Don't get blood on it or the diamond-clay will explode. And don't be too close when the seal breaks.'

'Wrap it in this.' Jasmin held out a scarf, beautiful colours in the silk. 'We have rather more blood outside our bodies than is strictly safe.'

Haram and Anria sprinted away towards the river, leaving their comrades behind them.

The Inoxit didn't take long to reach the spot where Cinome had touched the ground. They scuttled forward, their movements skittish and anxious.

Timon crouched in the branches of a tree, waiting for his moment. One of the Inoxit wandered too close and Timon took his chance. He dropped from his perch and landed upon the back of the creature, his sword stabbing deep. The Inoxit staggered, fell, but the others turned and swarmed over the badly injured Timon.

He screamed, 'Now!'

Jasmin threw the clay jar. It shattered. The explosion blasted another of the Inoxit into pieces, but, in amongst the trees, the rest of the Inoxit survived the blast and lay stunned for only a moment.

Not good enough, thought Timon, as his gaze darkened into death.

Jasmin barely had time to ready her blades before the Inoxit attacked.

The sound of the explosion reverberated across the moorland, telling Anria that her comrades were dead—an honourable sacrifice. Tussock grass beneath her feet, but she ran, lifting her knees high, behind

Haram. The gorge, where the entrance to the mine lay hidden, was just over the rise ahead of them, but the Inoxit would race across the moorland now their prey left the dampness of riverside.

'We'll make the mines,' Anria panted, 'but will we make the chamber?'

'No,' Haram said. His breath slow and easy.

'Have you any more of that diamond-clay?'

'Yes.' Haram handed over a small packet of the stuff. 'Not much.'

'Enough.'

'Use blood to trigger it.'

'I will.'

'And keep your mind quiet.'

The river thundered through the gorge. Haram followed Anria along the ledge, through the spray, until they reached the cave. Almost there; beyond the cave lay the spell-gold mines.

Spell-gold: a wondrous material which could both increase the power of a spell and insulate the world from its effects. Everybody thought the mine played out, empty of exploitable quantities of spell-gold; too much used up in the Mage Wars.

Haram had sensed the thinness of the magic and hunted deep into the mines until he found the beginnings of the dead zone and discovered what caused it.

A revelation.

Haram and Anria passed from light into darkness and the Scryer-marks around their eyes flared silver as their eyes adjusted. In their enhanced vision, the mine shone a ghostly green that extended into the darkness beyond. Wooden props and rails glimmered with a brighter shade of green, because once they were living wood.

A chittering echo from the darkness behind them. The Inoxit were already in the caves.

'I leave you here,' Anria said, pointing at a small side tunnel.

'Stay alive.'

'Unlikely.'

CHAPTER SEVEN

CINOME AWOKE IN THE DARKNESS of the mine. The magic was thin here. Why? Was this a dead zone? Yes; the magic draining away to nothingness. How had the slug found it? These Shonri were overbearing fools, but how had this one found a dead zone so close to her mountain? How had it remained hidden from her?

She groaned. This was a spell-gold mine. Magic should bubble, exuberant, from the rocks, from the spoil, from the edges of the darkness. Even with the metal mined clear, there should still be magic.

A shift, a door, a shift in space. Warm, moist air rising from dark depths below. Cinome couldn't see in this darkness and with the slug's grip upon her wrist, the pulsing power of his Scryer-marks upon her flesh, she couldn't extend her mind, her power, to sense what lay around her.

Another shift, another door, another drop down into a deeper level under the earth.

What was this?

A mind, a huge, complex, multifaceted mind surrounded her, pressed in upon her. The slug Haram released his grip upon her flesh, shifted her to a new, more comfortable—for him—position on his shoulder. Her magic was unblocked by Shonri electrum, but she could not break free, could not escape; the mind that surrounded her held her tight, squeezed her small.

Haram doubled his speed, running through the darkness. He was slug, Shonri, but he could see. That fool Basilard, to grant such power to mere slugs, untalented, tainted with mortality and morality, more dangerous than any of them knew.

Basilard broke his pact with the Twelve, tried to usurp the world, and died at the hands of these creatures. And many more Magi had died since his fall. The idiot.

Something scuttled down the wall and the wall lit up behind it. A glimmering, guttering, unearthly light.

Turmerix everywhere around her, but different to the ones she knew, their antennae long, waving, sensing, passing thoughts through the tumbled magnificence of their hive-mind. So vast, so strong, so rapidly flickering from thought to thought. She could feel it all, this pressing intellect; it held her still, close, tight within her stolen body.

She couldn't escape this.

Cinome screamed.

Haram laughed in the spectral light. 'Tempering,' he said as he continued to sprint through the cavernous space of the hive. 'You call it tempering.' His voice cold now, soft in the cavern, filled with sadness. 'When you cut away the Turmerixs' antennae to make them more tractable, you didn't know that you also cut them away from their hive, from their mind. But then, you didn't care, did you?'

In the little side tunnel near the mouth of the cave, Anria waited in the dark, a bandage around her arm from drawing blood for the trigger. Blood poured into a drinking cup and placed atop a pile of stones at the base of a pit prop. Under that pile of stones she had packed the diamond-clay tight against the wood.

She hefted the stone in her hand. A few more piled up in front of her, but if she missed with her first throw then she doubted she'd get a chance at a second.

Hush now.

They come.

Scenting the blood, one of the four remaining Inoxit stopped at the cup set atop the pile of rocks. It seemed to have difficulty understanding what it sensed. Its mind a weak little thing with so many parts of it dead.

Anria threw the rock. The Inoxit turned, caught the rock out of the air. It tilted its head to study it. Anria grabbed up another rock. Threw it with all the force of her Scryer-marks. It blurred through the air, past the turning Inoxit, struck the cup. Too much force. The blood splashed across the walls and the wood, but did any reach the diamond-clay?

The four Inoxit hissed at her out of the darkness. So fast. They'd be upon her soon. And she would die, knowing that she had failed Haram.

Then, a single drop of Anria's blood touched diamond-clay.

The explosion roared in the darkness of the cave.

As the ground shook, Haram pitched Cinome into the chamber through the round entrance hole. She landed heavily on the floor beneath. Her wrist broke in the darkness.

He heard it snap and laughed. 'Try to flee now, you mind-raping bitch.'

She couldn't flee, caught fast in the matrix of her stolen body. This chamber, the source of the dead zone, negated all magic. He waited, letting her find this out for herself.

'How is this so?' Cinome asked.

'Look around,' Haram said. 'See the whiteness of the walls, their shape. Oh, but you can't see in the dark, can you? Not this day.' He lighted a torch that flared brightly and threw the chamber into sharp relief. 'Magnesium torch. The Turmerix make them for us.'

'For you?'

'We have new allies in the fight, Cinome. You temper them whenever you find them, which makes you their enemy. So they ally to us. I kill those I find tempered, if I can. Release them from the shadow-life you have forced upon them.'

'Kill your allies?' Cinome asked, desperate for a diversion. Her Inoxit would come, she would be saved, it could not end like this.

'The tempered are not my allies. They live in hell. I release them.'

The chamber had pale walls, a high, domed roof, ridged but smooth and without any outcrops of splintered rock. There were two holes in the wall behind Haram. He glanced back to check the plug of spell-gold in one; the other had become the entrance for a time. The wall of the chamber under the holes extended away in a long, dark tunnel. More spell-gold glimmered around the teeth.

'Teeth,' Cinome gasped.

'This is the skull of a dragon. Nothing—no thought, no spell, no spirit—can pass through the bones of a dragon.'

'The dead zone,' Cinome said. 'This is the source of the dead zone.'

'It's the seed. When the Turmerix dug it out of the earth, they knew what they had found. They knew how dangerous it was and so they covered it in spell-gold. So much magic negated started an eddy in the flow. A dead zone grew here.' Haram leaned in close. 'Right next to your mountain.'

'Are you going to kill me now?'

'Yes.'

A sound outside the whiteness of the skull. Cinome exulted, 'Listen, slug, listen to my Inoxit coming to my rescue.' She laughed and pointed at the hole where a dragon's eye had once gleamed.

The Inoxit scuttled through and landed on the floor; twitching. They moved jerkily, stumbling into each other and the walls of the chamber.

'Lost your way, darlings?' Haram stretched. 'Being inside a dragon's skull will do that to you. Breaks the connections of your matrix. All alone in the dark, you foul little roaches.' He turned back to Cinome. 'What spell are they carrying?'

She hunched over against the back of the chamber, staring at the Inoxit in horror. She licked her lips, looked up at Haram. 'If I tell you, will you let me live?'

'No, I don't think so. I planned this entire outing just to kill you. You're a rancid stain on the world, the number of people you have subjugated. The spell would be a bonus but it won't save your life.'

'I know secrets,' Cinome said. 'I know—' She gasped, stared down at the dagger buried in her chest.

'Magnesium blade,' Haram said. 'I wanted to make sure you were dead.' He shook his head at her. 'You Magi could have made the world a place of joy and wonder. Instead you chose to tear it apart with your greed.'

'You're no different to me,' Cinome cried out with her last breath.

Haram kicked the staggering Inoxit out of his way, not bothering to kill them. He looked back at her.

'I am Shonri.'

He clambered out of the chamber as the magnesium blade ignited. The stench of burning flesh filled his nostrils. The moment he left the chamber, a group of long-bodied Turmerix began to close up the dragon's eye socket with glistening strands of spell-gold silk.

'One more down,' he muttered to himself. He wanted to talk to Felice, but she couldn't reach him here in the Turmerix hive. He had killed a member of the Twelve this day, but at what cost? An entire class of newborns killed. He should have waited. He should have called upon the Seven.

'So,' Anria called as she limped into the light. 'Have I passed?'

MEDINA LIFTED THE STRONGBOX ONTO THE BED. The map lay prepared and sanctified on the floor of her bedroom. She opened the strongbox and ran her fingers over the seven vials within. Her eyelids fluttered shut, her pulse accelerating, her nipples hardening.

Which one should be first?

Which of her conquests would fill her up with enough memories to power her spell-casting?

Ah, yes.

Her.

Oh yes, she had been so vigorous, so strong, a delightful first course for the power of Medina's craven sex.

Save Soldat for dessert. He had been so very sweet.

Medina removed her robe and stood naked for a moment, cradling the vial between her breasts. Then, with a delighted giggle, she knelt down upon the map.

It had taken a little while to get the map prepared, summer had long since passed into autumn, but still it was worth it.

For a perfect map.

Drawn with the juices of a slave cartographer. She sent him up in a Manta-ship, high, high above the world, to look down upon all below. Then she had his eyes, his brain, liquefied and poured upon the paper. A perfect map, very expensive, but she'd charge the Magi for its production.

Only one copy, of course.

They couldn't reproduce the map; they couldn't even have it drawn by another. The artist's eyes would dissolve and run out of their sockets if any were foolish enough to try. That, too, was part of the magic.

Ubiquity limited the price, so Medina always strove for uniqueness.

She kissed the vial, slid her tongue around its cold glass surface, remembered the taste of her, the touch of her, the smell of her. The crow-black liquid in the vial began to glow, to cast out its heat, warming the glass. Sweat poured from Medina's pores and splattered onto the surface of the map. The dots of sweat running, merging, forming traceries of paths taken and paths perhaps overlooked.

Sliding the vial over her naked body, across her full breasts, around her nipples, Medina breathed deeply, remembering. Her breath quickened, the speckles of her saliva dripped onto the map, running, merging, forming traceries.

The vial shuddered in her hand, awake, aware, remembering, flashing downwards between her parted thighs, up again over her navel, back down, and then up. Again and again it moved, just as she had teased, as she had played. Juices flowed onto the map. Running, merging.

Medina cried out in climax.

She knelt quietly for a moment, letting her heart rate slow, letting the traceries solidify into paths stained into the very fibre of the paper.

Gracefully, Medina stood and stepped away from the map. She studied it, head tilted to one side, drinking in the lines. She could read the lines like the lust in a lover's eyes, but others might not have such a skill.

No matter.

Not her problem.

They'd pay her anyway.

And if they couldn't decipher what they saw? Why then, they'd have to pay her twice.

She smiled, exchanged the vial for another. Was it wrong to love your work so much?

'Hello, you.' She kissed the vial and smirked.

CHAPTER NINE

I N THE CITY OF LIGHTS, as the first chill of winter crept into the air, Birsin followed his prey.

Not many Shonri could do what Birsin did. Most could quiet their minds, hide what they were from magical surveillance, but not many could hide their Scryer-marks, make them fade away within their skin, walk uncloaked with their faces uncovered, their skin on display for all the world to see. Not many could do that.

This made cities dangerous places for them.

In all other respects, Birsin made an unlikely-looking spy: squat, strong, his neck a triangle of solid muscle, his shoulders so broad he turned sideways to pass through narrow doorways, and his chest a powerful barrel of explosive strength. What was left of his blond hair he cropped close to the skull, exposing his much-scarred scalp to the winter sun, and he trimmed his greying beard and moustache to hide scarred lips. The facial hair surrounded his mouth like a wreath under his oft-broken nose. His blue eyes shifted colour, from the dark of the sea to the washed-out shade of a winter sky, as his emotions shifted on a tide of hate.

Out in the wilds his looks might cause comment, might cause people to remember him, but the cities were filled with men who looked like him: bravos, thugs, dangerous characters. He relied on this, on being just another odd man in the busy streets.

And so the cities became his hunting ground.

His quarry on this cold day, a man known as Longman, scurried like a frightened rodent through the thronging marketplace in the canyon streets of the City of Lights.

Longman's furtive manner made many a gaze linger on him for long moments. Merchants didn't care for people who sneaked around their wares without buying. Such behaviour made them reach for cudgels, on guard until the miscreant moved on. Common folk also didn't like people who wormed their way through the crowd. Such behaviour made them check their wallets and purses while hunching their shoulders and closing their fists. Market guards, though, quite liked such obviously disreputable characters, looked forward to a bit of blood sport and mayhem. Which, of course, gave the advantage to those miscreants with friends, who could take advantage of the commotion to steal whatever they desired.

Everybody noticed Longman but nobody noticed Birsin.

Birsin moved through the crowd in a languid manner, dropping a shoulder forward to slide effortlessly through gaps that opened up in the bustling throng. He could have battered his way through like a bull elephant, but that would create a disturbance. That would create a wake of curses behind him, of eyes watching him, seeing him, remembering his face, his build, his manner. No, quiet was best. Stealth was a hunter's way.

At the edge of the marketplace, Longman darted into a tavern. A disreputable place, much frequented by guards and criminals alike. Birsin rested against a wall opposite the bolthole and studied its challenges, dirty windows, unwashed patrons sitting outside in the weak morning sun—already drunk and leering at passers-by.

He weighed his options. If he walked in through that front door then all eyes would turn towards him. A silence would fall as the regulars noted an unknown face. Hard eyes that knew too much of banal brutality would study him with care. Some of the bravos might even step up to test his mettle. His grey beard and balding scalp might make them think that he wasn't what he appeared, that he wasn't dangerous.

Drink makes fools of men who should know better.

Not the front door then, but he needed a distraction if he meant to slip around the back and recapture Longman's trail.

Birsin glanced around. This end of the market, notwithstanding the seedy tavern—and maybe because of it—sold luxury items and gewgaws for those with too much money and too little sense. He smiled. The market stall selling magicked fireworks to folk who wished to celebrate the winter solstice would do nicely as a distraction.

The Magi had broken the world, destroyed all that came before in their lust for power, for dominion over humanity, and still people, the common folk, bought the petty little baubles of apprenticed Magi and laughed gaily at the sparkling lights in the sky. City folk, sophisticated, jaded, corrupt and wilfully ignorant in their pursuit of a quiet and prosperous life; a life dominated by tittle-tattle and opinions formed by salacious hypocritical news-rags that called the Shonri enemy and lifted the Magi and their sycophants into paragons of virtue and worth.

Birsin rested his hand on the edge of the merchant's stall. Delicate as a lover, he allowed the Scryer-marks on his hand to flare into brightness for a moment before they faded back into his tanned skin. He hid the flare behind the back of an overstuffed matron, who argued with some other woman about the rightness of the mayor's decision to sell the homeless and the destitute into slavery.

Both women agreed that such an act of barbarity was a good idea, a capital one, they said. They only argued about what the money raised upon the backs of the weak should be used for. One wanted to build a new city hall because the old one had become a little shabby; the other wanted to bolster the army for these were dangerous times. Both opinions formed by competing news-rags that supported different factions on the city council.

Birsin gritted his teeth: as if any of that mattered. The Magi ruled this world. A new city hall didn't make the city any more liberated and the size of an army made up of mere humans didn't make the city any more secure. The Magi employed creatures of nightmare in their forces. The Magi allowed the mayor to rule the city purely because they couldn't be bothered to deal with the tedious nature of such management. The Twelve handed down their edicts and the mayor implemented them. These facts hidden behind the lies and misdirection of propaganda.

Besides, the Pyramid was all that really mattered in this city and that was guarded by things inhuman. Even now, the Raptors of Zarak flew through the sky above the city, gazing down with terrible eyes to see anything that threatened the Pyramid's security. *That* was the centre of this city, not the shabby little city hall with its bumbling bureaucrats and fumbling politicians.

People were such fools.

Those eagle eyes in the sky above were a true danger to Birsin, but he had to move quickly, to risk exposure for a moment. He had used his power, let the marks flare, and now he must leave that spot before the magical protection nullified by his touch became a worm of explosive potential spreading amongst the fireworks.

He strode across the street to the alleyway alongside the tavern.

Self-lighting fuses lit, sparking and smoking. The merchant yelled a warning, threw himself backwards over a broken wall. People turned, confused, and looked across at the stall. Some realised the danger, rushed away, cried out warnings of their own. A quick-thinking guard yelled orders.

The explosion seemed to stop the world for a moment in a ripping blast of heat and noise. Glass shattered in the windows of the tavern. A shrapnel storm tore through the drunken patrons.

Birsin spotted Longman running away from the back of the tavern towards the old warehouse district down by the river.

Which was exactly where he wanted him to be.

He quieted his thoughts, keeping his Scryer-marks hidden because of the Raptor's gaze, and sprinted after the fleeing Longman. A risk? Yes, but many people were running away from the explosion, fleeing from the Kirruk lizardmen guards that the Magi were sure to send to keep order. The city council retrospectively rubber-stamped anything the Magi's forces did, no matter how vile. It was always best to get away from any disturbance in the smooth running of the City of Lights.

Birsin caught Longman by the broken door of a derelict warehouse which had lost its custom when the sea-trade was terminated by the war that left oceans too dangerous to cross.

Longman turned, brandishing a dagger; even rats will fight when cornered. Birsin slapped the dagger aside and threw Longman through the rotten wood of a door, then calmly followed him into the gloom.

'You've been avoiding me, my friend,' Birsin said.

'I need more time.'

'Time's up.' Birsin gripped the smaller man by the throat, his voice harsh, his eyes as dark as the storm-tossed sea. 'What did you discover?'

'They'll kill me if I tell you.' Longman pulled at Birsin's hand, but he didn't have the strength to move those fingers; he was, after all, only human. 'They have a Lamia, you fool. She'll see what is in my mind. They'll kill me. I need more money. I need to get away from this place. I need to hide.'

'A fair point,' Birsin said, 'but I've paid you already. Tell me what you know and I will see if it's worth a little extra to help you on your way.'

'You promise?'

'Don't be ridiculous, Longman. Tell me.' Birsin closed his grip slightly around Longman's throat. A testing little squeeze. He could crush the man's throat if he closed his hand fully.

Longman gasped, struck at Birsin's face, tried to push him away.

Birsin relaxed his grip. 'Tell me.'

Longman sucked in air and managed to splutter, 'They have a map.'

'A map?'

'Some magicked thing. It shows the tracks of the Shonri upon the land.'

'Shonri?' Birsin shook Longman by the throat.

'Aye, those murderous scum. Don't you understand? This information will see you burned at the stake. It'll see me burn alongside you. I have to get away.'

'Where is the map?'

'In the Pyramid. Zarak keeps it safe for the Twelve.' Longman's eyes darted, seeking an escape route.

'Does he now? How accurate is it?'

'They don't know. They can't read it properly. The mapmaker is coming to show them how to read it.'

Birsin raised a scarred eyebrow. 'When will this mapmaker arrive?'

'I don't know. I'm only a steward. I only know what I overhear.'

Birsin paused, thought for a moment. 'You'd better disappear, Longman.' He closed his hand.

Still in the gloom of the derelict warehouse, with Longman's corpse cooling on the floor beside him, Birsin opened his mind to the connection.

'We have a problem, Felice,' he sent.

Chapter Ten

I T WAS A MISTAKE to set such a one on the trail of Medina.

She hurried along the pulsating corridor in the centre of the Worm-train. A creature force-grown by magic until it reached a kilometre in length and forty meters in diameter. Passengers sat in crystal-walled compartments in the Worm's sides; the poor creatures carved open by magic to hold the passenger compartments and then twisted by magic to form the long tubular corridor extending along their centres; a corridor that contracted and expanded as the creatures undulated along the slime-bud-walled tunnels.

Some Mage had set a Gilbon-tracker on her trail. Probably stupid little Calderan, who had offered a second payday for the same work, the same map, and yet didn't trust her to come to the money.

How little he understood her.

The corridor-tube contracted forcefully as the Worm made the turn into the final tunnel leading to the City of Lights. Medina crouched in the corridor to let the contraction pass and sensed the Gilbon close behind her, hiding in shadows. In this well-lit corridor there should be no shadows. Medina tutted: poor little Gilbon had no other defence.

Gilbons had the ability to cloud the mind, but Medina rarely bothered to use hers. Instead, she relied on instinct and the emotional flux of the magic flowing around her. She didn't plan, as such, but simply saw opportunities arise and then acted upon her nature. Medina rarely thought of anything beyond what to do next.

And then she acted.

It had kept her alive when she should have died, this chaotic approach to the world. When the Shonri rebelled, she escaped their duplicitous attack by the smallest of margins, but she escaped. While her sisterhood died, she survived because she didn't think, or plan, or hesitate. She simply reacted and became Medina.

When the Shonri started to come to her for healing, she took their lust, their heat, the touch of their Scryer-marks, everything that made them what they were, and bottled it, enchanted it, made it her own. Not because she thought about the power she held in the palm of her hand, but simply because she could.

It pleased her.

The contraction passed along the corridor and she stood once more, with a deft twist of the hips to give the Gilbon an eyeful of what lay beneath her skirt.

Still enough time; an hour yet before they arrived at the terminus.

Gilbons were humans merged with Inoxit insects in a foul concoction of magic—and the human stock most capable of accepting the touch of an insect into their spirit had proved to be the Enasi sex slaves; their minds already warped, their souls already diminished by the breeding of their particular talents, Enasi would have sex with anything, anyone, any creature, for the amusement of their owners. Medina had once seen one broken open by the attentions of a Callort fighting pair. The eight-foot-tall Callorts were proportional in all things and she'd laughed as the Enasi screamed and gibbered for more, even as his blood pooled upon the floor where he lay.

An experiment, no more. She had simply wanted to see what an Enasi would do for those that commanded them.

Lust is a powerful thing.

And Gilbons were born to it.

Medina turned, looked directly at the Gilbon—hiding in his mind-cast shadow—and crooked a seductive finger. 'Come along now.'

She slipped into an empty compartment, sprawled across the velvet-covered seat with her legs open, inviting, and smiled as the shadow paused beyond the door.

'I can see you,' she crooned. 'Can you see me?'

The shadow flowed away and revealed the creature. Nurtured on a soup of neurons, capable of seeing into the minds of others, of obscuring their thoughts, of trailing them with dreadful tenacity, the Gilbon was a sallow-skinned being with a head too big for his body.

Medina sighed.

This would be a trial.

Still.

Needs must.

'What is your name, Gilbon?' she asked softly.

'Gilbert,' the creature answered, with the whispering voice of his kind.

Medina groaned. 'That is a poor joke, Gilbert the Gilbon. So, Calderan is your master?'

'Yes.' A long hiss.

Medina sipped from the edges of Gilbert's mind. He could see nothing in this woman's soul except lust for him. He knew that he should not, that his orders were to follow, to remain unseen, to await other orders, but she could see him, she wanted him.

He couldn't refuse that.

His master used him as a weapon of torture sometimes. A creature with no morals, bred to pleasure others, crossbred to see into the minds of others with an insect's amoral coldness, made a useful torturer, but Calderan didn't let him pleasure willing partners, didn't let him give the gratification his Enasi side craved above all else.

Medina let her native lust bubble upwards as the nasty little sneak Gilbert slipped into her.

He did have skills. She moaned and moved. He took the wrong memory from her mind and became gentle, soft, a generous lover. She almost ate him alive at that point, but instead thrust the memory of the Callort into his mind, force-feeding him the degradation.

Anger flared in Gilbert. She took sustenance from its heat. He thrust harder, his face contorted, the washed-out grey of his eyes almost invisible as he strained.

The climax rose within her from the web of pain. Uplifting her, giving her the power to reach into Gilbert's brain and crush his scrawny mind.

On top of the creature now, straddling him, looking into his slack-jawed face, his dulled eyes. He still thrust, still increased the connection, making the power flow, making him hers.

'Isn't this nice?' Medina hissed.

Gilbert couldn't reply. He was lost, spinning upon the noose of her appetites. The words snarled in his throat. He was she, she was he, no gap in between, no space for him to hide. Bile flooded his mouth and she made him swallow it back.

'I'm not kissing that mouth.' Medina shuddered, a little more, ah… there; he was hers now. Always useful to have a spy within the enemy camp.

The Worm-train slicked itself to a stop at just about the same time as Medina.

She adjusted her clothing. 'You'll hide this recruitment from your master.'

'Yes, mistress,' Gilbert said.

'You'll come when I call. You're mine now.'

'Yes, mistress.'

Satisfied, Medina walked away from her newfound slave. Now to go to the Pyramid and fleece these Magi for as much as she could get.

Gilbert hid in shadow for shame.

CHAPTER ELEVEN

THEY CALLED IT THE CITY OF LIGHTS.

The Shonri knew better; Soldat knew the darkness beneath the grandeur of the illuminations.

The city sprawled, cascading over the hills, along the meandering banks of a slow-moving river. The homes of the high and mighty, standing alone within walled gardens, topped some of the hills. Houses of stone and steel with hand-blown glass windows that reflected the lights' glimmer into the sky. Their owners, men and women of grace and favour, looked down across their great city with arrogant eyes and haughty superiority.

On other hills—even hills right next to the stone-cast magnificence of the mighty houses of the wealthy—shantytowns of stone, wood, broken boxes, piled-up rocks, with canvas sheets flapping in the wind and streets running with excrement, swarmed upwards into the night. Above these disordered townships rose the houses of the gang leaders, the masters of the shambles. Brutal men and women with eyes empty of all empathy and pity.

The poor, the rich, and every strata in between, mixed together on those hillsides, in the canyon streets between the hills, on the broad floodplain of the meandering river. Shopping, fornicating, drinking away the night hours. A way of life encouraged by the Magi, codified by the Magi, to keep the people helpless and reliant on the Magi for their protection and security.

The broken world outside the city walls belonged to others but here, in the city, the lights flared into the dark. Torches burned, sending tendrils of smoke into the sky from within the flammable confines of the shantytowns. Witch-globes floated above the townhouses of the rich, casting soft-edged illumination that could sharpen into devastating brightness if ever the garden walls were threatened. The canyon streets lit by lines of glow-poles: tall, standing beacons of Mage-crafted lustre to lighten the steps of their serfs. All of them serfs really—for no one was free in the City of Lights. They all served the Magi, though some were better than others at lying to themselves about this.

Shop frontages lay open to the night air, smelling of spices, herbs, leather, and wood. Taverns, stinking of stale beer, stale smoke and stale blood welcomed any who could pay—until the money ran out. A babbling, fuming corruption of sound infested the streets. People talked, argued, haggled, sang drunken songs to forget the breaking of the world. They whispered sweet nothings to gain the solace of a warm body for the cold winter's night. This broken edge of humanity, cast out from freedom, from beauty, from all they had once held truthful, because the Magi came.

And there, off-centre within the mass of the city's stumbling demesne, within a loop of solemn river, cold and clean in the rank night air, stood the rearing, flat-topped Pyramid.

Windows, perfect panes of flat glass, let the light flood out of the building. So many windows glared into the dark, breaking the pure form of the Pyramid into steps of light, leading the eye upwards to the flat top of the structure, where the light died to allow the auburn-feathered raptor-guards to roost for the night.

At night, the city had other guards—a mistake.

Down amongst the lights, figures moved through the thronging crowds. Seven cloaked figures, their skins hidden. They mostly walked alone, although two guided a horse-drawn wagon piled high with things hidden under canvas.

Seven cloaked figures slipped between the drunken, loud, belligerent city folk. Six of the figures stepped just so to avoid confrontation, to avoid notice, to avoid discovery. Seven Shonri entered the city from six different directions but all headed for one quiet spot amongst the hubbub.

Six kept their minds hushed, quiet in the dark, but still the glow-poles flickered for a moment when they passed. The Raptor flock would have seen those flickering trails along the city streets. Their sharp eyes would have spotted the light-wakes of the Shonri. But Raptors were bred from eagles and roosted during the night.

It must be said that some Shonri were better at hiding what they were than others, at hiding their minds, at holding their Scryer-marks placid. Six of these Seven were Old Ones, the original Shonri, all that were left of those that rebelled. One was newborn; but even she had more control over her mind's turmoil than Soldat.

Soldat the indomitable, the one who saw the way to freedom, the one who led three hundred Shonri against their master Basilard, rarely bothered to quiet his mind.

That was not his way.

He kept his cloak closed, with the spell-gold cloth hiding him as it hid the others, because of the others. Without them, without the war, he would have fought his way into this city, killed any that stood against him, let loose a cry of freedom and died there upon the steps of the Pyramid. He didn't care about life or death, but he did care about victory and the lives of his comrades.

So he strode through the crowded streets with his cloak closed and the hood covering his head, but his deep gaze swept across the people surrounding him, his strong hands tightened on the blades at his belt, as his native anger mounted. The glow-poles started to dim when he passed. They flickered when the hushed Scryer-marks of the other Shonri slipped along the streets, but they dimmed to almost nothing when wrathful Soldat strode past.

The people of the city looked up, puzzled by the shadows falling across their faces, fearful of the shadows that lay in the catacombs beneath their feet, but the glow-poles re-energised once Soldat moved on and the people shrugged, laughed and returned to their hedonistic distractions.

A squad of Kirruk lizardmen noted the dimming poles and reacted as they were prone to do in such situations. They battered their way through the crowd towards Soldat. Screams of pain, cries of anger, of outrage, from the people, but the six hulking lizardmen ignored it all in their single-minded pursuit of the source of this darkness in the midst of the City of Lights.

They had their orders: darkness must never fall.

Soldat smiled and moved swiftly towards them. He let them see the flash of his Scryer-marks within the gloom of his hood and then darted down an alleyway.

They followed of course, for Kirruk are not the most intelligent of creatures, not intelligent enough to send a runner to warn of a Shonri loose in the city. They simply gave chase. Soldat waited in the alley.

'Hello,' he said. The scythes in his hands slashed through the air, through lizard flesh, leaving trails of green blood splattered over the walls of the alley. Sweeping low, then high, from left and then right, his feet kicking, his strong shoulders used as battering rams, and still the scythes cut.

It didn't take long.

Soldat walked out of the alleyway, leaving the scattered corpses of the lizardmen behind him, with not a trace of green blood upon his cloak.

And the lights shone undimmed in his wake.

CHAPTER TWELVE

S HE STOOD WAITING WHEN HARAM closed the warehouse doors behind the wagon. Slim as a willow with eyes the colour of honey between long lashes. Her cloak thrown back over her shoulders to reveal her weapons: blades, long and short; a quiver of arrows on her right hip, a collapsed bow upon her left; sharpened stars on straps across her torso, stars she could throw with efficiency and speed—a peal of death through bloody air.

Felice.

Felice the Conduit. She held the touch of the Seven in her mind and connected them as a family no matter how far apart they roamed. In the gloom of the warehouse she kept her mind hushed, her Scryer-marks dim, but active enough to connect all to all in a single circuit. She had guided them all here, to this safe place, this sanctuary against detection in the City of Lights, after Birsin sent out the call.

Haram barely noticed Birsin standing beside Felice, but the Hidden One, the Shonri who hid in plain sight and fought the war with the guile and duplicity of a spy, said, 'Soldat's killed a squad of Kirruk.'

Haram snarled into the darkness. 'Is he here yet?'

'Not yet, but he's not far away.'

Felice tilted her head like a bird studying a worm and asked, 'Who is this?'

'Anria,' Haram said.

'A novice?' Birsin asked, unimpressed. He led the horses away from the wagon after Anria released them from the harness.

'No more,' Haram said. 'She helped me kill Cinome.'

Felice switched her gaze to Haram. 'You don't kill a Lamia. You know this. You can only bottle up their soul in a place where it cannot find a host.'

'Whatever. She'll not escape that bottle.'

Felice smiled at Anria. 'Come here, child.'

The marks around Anria's eyes glowed silver in the dark. 'I'm not a child.'

'To me you are… to us. Longevity gives us the eyes of the old behind the faces of the young.'

'Does she always talk like this?' Anria asked.

Haram shrugged. 'She's Felice.' He set about untying the canvas covering the wagon bed.

'What have you brought?' Birsin asked.

'Gifts from the Turmerix.' Haram pulled back the spell-gold cloth hidden beneath the canvas.

Anria's bravado died away. 'Felice?' A tremor in her voice.

Haram looked up from showing Birsin a heavy crossbow, doubled-steel arms that could drive a bolt straight through the chest of a stone-skinned Callort. 'Aye, the Conduit.'

The Conduit, the communicator, cursed by Basilard's magic to be a line of communication between the Shonri at war. One of many communicators amongst the ranks of the late and unlamented Basilard's Shonri forces, but Felice was the only Conduit to join the rebellion. She had killed her sisters with mind-blasts of power along those very same lines of telepathic connection.

'Come here, Anria,' Felice said, a little louder.

Birsin picked up a repeating cross bow. The magazine lay atop the stock; snapping it back and forth drew back the string, cocked the weapon, and dropped another bolt into the groove. Only a Shonri could hope to use such a weapon. The strength and dexterity required was beyond that of any normal human.

'Magnesium-tipped bolt,' Haram said, 'or diamond-clay, but you can't mix one with the other in the same magazine.'

'How about folded steel?' Birsin asked.

'Come here, Anria,' Felice said again.

'I have some.' Haram nodded. 'Zarak's armour?'

'Aye, a magazine loaded with fire and armour-piercing might be just what we need.' Birsin glanced at Anria; the novice looked scared. As well she might.

Haram shrugged. 'Better with the clay. Punch a hole, drop an explosive bolt through the gap.'

'All three would be best.'

'You'd have to place two steel bolts between the clay and the fire,' Haram said. 'Only ten bolts to a magazine. And I'd be careful not to drop the damn thing if I were you.'

Birsin scratched his ear. 'Aye, well, I'll think on it.' He pointed at a large brassbound trunk. 'What's that?'

Haram grinned. 'That's something special.' He glanced across at Anria.

Who had thrown back her cloak, settled her shoulders, and now walked towards the legendary Felice on steady feet.

That took real courage; but she wouldn't feel such fear if she had seen Felice, her back arched, the dappled twilight of the forest on her nakedness, her head thrown back in orgasm. Haram shook the memory away.

'I remember it too,' Felice sent into the darkness of his mind.

He sent nothing in return. After the death... after the murder of her sisters, Felice fled into the wilderness and disappeared for two decades, lost to the war. Haram had searched for her, a desperate time, but found nothing. She hadn't wanted him to find her.

Then she returned, still Shonri, still a Conduit for the thoughts of others, but no longer Haram's lover. He often wondered if she blamed him for persuading her to join the rebellion, not knowing what she'd do; he'd thought that she might try to subvert her sisters, but she'd taken another route.

'There is no blame,' Felice sent. *'There was no other way.'*

'But still I wonder.'

'I know.'

Anria faced Felice.

Felice smiled, her head tilted, her eyes holding Anria's gaze. She raised her hands. Anria shied away from the touch of those fingers, but Felice's gaze held her static.

'Don't fight it,' Haram whispered into the dark.

The pain started where Felice's fingers touched Anria's scalp, a driving pain, digging deeper, stronger, blazing through Anria's mental barriers, into her, into all that made her Anria.

'Who are you?'
'I am Anria.'
'What are you?'
'I am Shonri.'
'What were you before?'

The memories flowered into the connection between the two Shonri. Memories Anria had thought safely hidden, buried under her anger and grief.

A child grows up in a cold family, a wealthy family, a family of courtiers to the Magi. The child is talented, a musician, it is assumed that she will one day play for the Magi in the halls across the land.

Her family were merchants, powerful in their own way. They turned their faces against the suffering of others. Her father, a bluff man of raging thirst, drank too much and talked too much when in his cups. Her mother, a skeletal, fragile woman, was much given to fainting spells and spent many days abed. Her brothers, mean-spirited and vicious, her sisters, judgemental and shrewish. All despised Anria for her gift, the music that made her special.

An old story; serving the Magi in the degradation of humanity took its toll upon the human spirit.

Then one day her father, in his cups, said too much to the wrong person and the eyes of the Magi turned away from the family. No income. No protection. Too many enemies. For all were enemies when in the employ of the Magi; all vied to prosper, to advance, to survive.

The fall.

The streets.

The poor, whom her family turned their faces from, took pleasure in the revenge. They extracted the wealth from Anria's parents and returned their cruelty with interest.

Anria struggled in Felice's grasp. This wasn't right. She didn't want to see this again, to live this again.

'Stop, please, stop.'
'This was your city?'
'Yes.'
'You were born here?'
'Yes.'

'You will be useful.'

Felice released the gasping Anria and wiped tears from the youngster's eyes, tears that Felice shared. 'You're joined to me now,' she whispered. 'You're part of the connection.'

Anria slapped her across the face.

'We'd best get the wagon unloaded,' Birsin said.

****

Medina closed her eyes. Ah, Felice was in the city. She smiled at the memory of the first time. Her fingers traced a line through the sweat slicking her naked flesh. Remembering…

Somebody else here?

In this room?

Medina's eyes snapped open.

'You are required,' a man said. He stood in the doorway, dressed in cloth finely woven but without the expensive quality of a Mage's garments. An obvious lesser Mage.

During the day, mirrored channels served in place of windows to light this suite, deep within the heart of the Pyramid. At night those same channels glowed with a different light, but still bright enough for vision, helped by the walls, brightly painted to capture and reflect every ray.

Just before the dawn, the light fluttered fitfully and gave up more heat as it cleansed itself of wasted energy. Cool air sighed through other channels, but still it was overly warm within the suite.

Medina didn't mind the heat, she'd chosen these rooms; she wanted to be close to the centre of the Pyramid, close to her goal. Yet this man thought to treat her as a prisoner.

That wouldn't do. That wouldn't do at all.

'I didn't give you leave to enter my chamber.' She spoke with a silk-soft voice and looked at the Mage. Ah, Patran. It was to be expected that he would dare this trespass.

'This chamber belongs to the Twelve,' Patran said.

'Not when I'm in it.' Medina rose sinuously to her feet, naked and sensuous in the sighing air.

'Witch, you have no power over me.'

'Just because you prefer men, don't presume immunity.' Medina lifted her dress from the floor, a thing of silk, so fine that it almost didn't seem to exist at all.

Patran sneered at this display of womanly grace. Such softness. Hips like the wide curving edges of a bay instead of narrow as a river. A waist so slender that he could encircle it with two hands, not ridged with muscle and pulsing under his grasp. The heavy pendulous breasts with their large nipples, not the flat expanse of a man's chest, strong and powerful. Her skin, so smooth, so hairless, so… Patran became aware of his erection.

'I smell nicer too,' Medina said. She bent over to wind the straps of her sandals around her calves and looked up at him through her dishevelled hair. 'Enter my chambers again without my leave and I will eat your soul.'

Chapter Thirteen

A COLD, BLEAK WINTER'S DAWN came to the City of Lights. As the sun rose, sending light along the channels into the heart of the Pyramid, Soldat walked through the streets of the city with his cloak closed and his eyes aware.

On the flat top of the Pyramid, the Raptors stirred. Great beaks lifted into the light, scenting the air. Great wings, longer across than double the height of a tall man, flexed in the weak winter sunlight. Great talons that could crush the head of a Callort scrabbled on the dark-veined marble. Golden feathers ruffled softly in the rising breeze. Dark, deep-set eyes peered out across the city. The Raptors called to the dawn with a deep, mournful song.

Soldat heard that cry to the dawn and cursed softly.

On the streets of the city the lights that blazed all night, keeping away the darkness, blinked out one by one. Glow-poles faded back to dull unreflective grey, witch-globes descended to the ground and flickered into darkness, torches hissed as slaves raced around the streets extinguishing them with metal cups.

As the sun rose, the streets began to clear. Raptors fed on the undefended and, until they ate their fill, very few citizens ventured out into the light.

Soldat alone walked through the scurrying slaves. The poor expendable human chattels, desperate to get their task completed so that they could return to the sanctuary of their master's pens, didn't even look at the cloaked figure of Soldat. They'd seen Raptor-feed before; people who simply gave up on life and walked out into the dawn; people who risked a saunter through the dawn-light in an act of bravado, on a wager, for a dare. The deluded, the foolish and the brave. Whatever the reasons, there were always enough people to keep the Raptors fed.

Soldat had no wish to tangle with the Raptors. Not this morning. He'd laid down his marker by killing the Kirruk and the ambiguous nature of that act would leave the city unsteady. No need to lessen its impact by leaving dead Raptor flesh on the very doorstep of the Shonri's hideaway.

He couldn't run, though, not while there were slaves around who might catch a glimpse of his Scryer-marks.

The Raptors ceased their mournful chorus and, with a sigh of feathers, took to the air. They swooped low over the city, gaining speed, mighty wings outstretched, talons tucked under their tail feathers. They swept over the rooftops, calling harshly, before, with languid flaps, they climbed high above the city to wheel and swoop—to hunt.

Soldat, the streets empty at last, sprinted along the alleyways, keeping his nerve, never looking up. If he heard the approach of a Raptor, then he'd turn and cut it from the air; but such an act would be disastrous.

'This way,' Felice called into his mind. *'Run harder, you have only seconds left.'*

There was an open space in front of the warehouse, trees masking its edges. Soldat raced across the rubble-strewn ground with inhuman agility.

A hungry Raptor spotted movement under the trees and dived lower to investigate.

Soldat stopped moving.

'I need a distraction,' he mind-sent.

'Haram will provide one,' Felice replied.

Two horses burst from the warehouse, driven out by powerful slaps upon their rumps. Blinking in the light, the horses smelled Raptors on the wind and bolted.

The Raptor spotted the horses and swooped after them.

Soldat waited a moment longer before completing his run to the warehouse unmolested.

'Dammit, Soldat,' Haram snapped. 'Those horses didn't deserve that.'

'I was…' Soldat shrugged '…delayed.'

'I know. I heard. I thought this was supposed to be a secret mission?'

Soldat gazed at his friend, his mouth lifting into a smile. 'No, not secret… just covert.'

****

Medina sashayed into Zarak's chamber, built in the exact centre of the Pyramid. She could feel a power pulsing through this room, which had nothing to do with the four Magi waiting for her.

Calderan stood by the basalt slab in the centre of the chamber. Fire fumed sulphurous in his mind. A powerful Mage, but unable to make creatures of his own, his talent too hot, too fickle, too voracious. He needed an entourage of lesser Magi to control his armies and servants. But he could still melt this entire Pyramid to a slumped heap of glass if he so chose, and so the other Magi granted him respect.

Rin stood with her back to Medina. Her ancient bones might well creak under her heavy shawl, but Rin possessed real power. Power enough to make creatures of her own, if not of her own designs; she used templates stolen from other Magi or purchased with favours. Medina smirked; Rin's own designs always failed, for she didn't have the imagination to make them work. But Rin did command an army and was ferocious in the defence of her position amongst the Twelve. She was also as treacherous as a snake.

And then there was Zarak, a true maker, a creator. As old as Rin, he kept his body young with the distilled life force of human and creature alike. His armour was heavy, ornate, bejewelled, but Medina wasn't fooled. Those jewels were spell charms; the metal had a high Scryer-silver content, and the ornate fluting channelled that magical energy into a shield that could also be a weapon.

What was this? A new face. A young face. The touch of a mind questing against Medina's. A Lamia, then. A replacement for Cinome amongst the Twelve? No matter. Medina slapped the probing thought away with a spell-strike of her own.

The Lamia hissed, drew back, her cornflower-blue eyes narrowed in fury.

'Leave her, Sora,' Zarak snapped. 'You were warned.' The shafts of light spearing down from the diagonal ceiling of the chamber left half his face in shadow.

'She is but a Witch.' Sora stood close to Calderan beside the shining black stone dominating the centre of the chamber. The oblong seemed to be made of a single block of solid basalt, but Medina knew it was much more than just rock.

'She is Medina.' Rin lowered herself into a high-backed chair. 'She matched Cinome in strength and you, Sora, are not Cinome.'

'Not yet,' Calderan added hastily.

Had the old goat found a new glove to cover his aging flesh?

Medina stretched in a shaft of sunlight, almost as if she showered in its luminescence, reaching up, tipping her head back, closing her eyes, but keeping her awareness needle-sharp.

Calderan's gaze hungry upon her. Sora's gaze angry upon Calderan. Rin's laugh, a harsh sound filled with fluid.

Medina curtseyed to the old woman and sat across the basalt from her on another high-backed chair.

Unlike her suite of rooms—the suite of rooms she always used when she visited with Zarak, the suite of rooms he kept ready for her even though her visits were infrequent and irregular—unlike her suite, the central chamber glowered rather than glowed.

If anything, even more light flooded in from the shafts high in the slanted walls and sloping ceiling, through transparent channels carved into the very floor, but the walls of the chamber soaked up the light, absorbed it, gave off no reflection. There was real power here and Medina basked in it.

As she always did.

'Where are the others?' she asked.

The good humour left Rin's features. 'They refused to come. They said you'd already been paid. They saw no need to pay you twice.'

'You pay me for two separate tasks. I made you the map. It shows the paths of the Shonri as clear as daylight.'

'But we cannot read it,' Calderan snarled.

'You didn't ask to be able to read it. You merely asked for the map. You should've been more specific.'

'Yes,' Zarak said. 'He should have been. I would have been.'

'I know.' Medina licked her lips. 'You're always so very specific.'

Zarak turned his head away and called for drinks, a strangled quality to his voice.

'Do you sleep with every man who crosses your path?' Sora asked, her pleasant tone no disguise for her intended insult.

'Not everyone.' Medina glanced at Calderan. 'I do have standards.'

She let her gaze drift slowly across Sora's long-limbed, athletic body. 'And not only men.' A blush brightened Sora's cheeks and Medina grinned. 'Lamias are—'

A lesser Mage in armour much like Zarak's own, but of inferior quality, hurried into the chamber. He whispered something in Zarak's ear.

Zarak's hand slapped the basalt slab and the sound of flesh on stone echoed around the chamber. 'What! In my city?'

'Is anything wrong?' Medina asked.

****

Anria's hands still shook as she helped Birsin and Haram to unload the wagon while Soldat conferred with Felice. The Conduit had dredged up Anria's past and the pain that lay there.

'You're the first new member of the connection in over twenty years,' Haram said as he handed her a bundle of cloth. 'Most are found wanting when Felice touches their minds.'

'We're all Shonri.' Anria handed the cloth down to Birsin, who passed it on to somebody lower in the tunnels under the warehouse. Anria knew what lay at the end of those tunnels. A good hiding place, but dangerous in the dark.

'Some don't have the clarity of purpose,' Birsin said. 'They fight, they die, but they won't do all that is needed.'

'They won't tear down the world,' Anria translated.

'This isn't a world.' Haram handed her a heavy crossbow. 'It's a prison for the soul.'

'A torture chamber.' Soldat's consultation with Felice had ended and he touched Anria on the shoulder. 'Welcome.' He glanced up at Haram. 'I'll get Lorak. None of us is strong enough to carry that mysterious trunk through the passageways below unaided.'

Anria stepped back against the wall to let Soldat pass.

Lorak the Strong. Anria could not quite believe that she stood amongst this legendary company, linked to them. Soldat, who began the revolt, planned it, commanded the forces. Felice, who had killed her sisterhood and still connected one to all. Birsin, the last of the Hidden Ones, the spy Shonri, they said that he snuck into the middle of Basilard's camp, struck the Mage's head from his shoulders with a single blow, chucked that head on a pyre of Shonri dead, ended the rebellion and began the war.

'Up or down?' Haram asked. 'Anria!'

She returned to the moment. 'What?'

'Up or down?'

'I—'

'There'll be room for no other when Lorak enters the tunnel. Too late. Up you come.'

Anria scrambled up onto the floor of the warehouse, Birsin close behind her.

Then Lorak emerged from the tunnel. Birsin was broad across the shoulders, Haram was strong in the arms, Soldat was tall and powerful, but Lorak…

Lorak was not much taller than Soldat, but his shoulders extended like flat planes from the cowl of muscle beneath his huge skull. No neck to speak of, built like a bull, shaped like a bull, all meat and gristle. He looked as if he could pick up the wagon with one hand, let alone the trunk that lay upon it. There was no fat on him. His thighs were as wide around as Haram's waist.

'You Anria?' he rumbled from somewhere deep within his massive chest.

'Yes,' Anria squeaked. She got her voice under control. 'Yes.'

'Welcome to the family.' The angles of his face realigned themselves into something approaching a smile. He slapped her lightly, for him, on the shoulder. 'I'm Lorak.'

'Well she didn't think you were me, now did she?' A tiny woman whose head barely reached Lorak's breastbone followed him out of the tunnel. 'Hello, Anria, I'm Quila.'

Anria smiled despite the tingling in her shoulder.

'Don't worry,' Quila said, 'the bruise will fade in a few days.'

Quila, the Clever One, who had magic of her own to rival the Magi's.

'I'm…' Anria licked dry lips. 'Um… very glad to meet you.'

Quila studied her with eyes so dark that they seemed to have no iris at all, just pupils dilated to catch every particle of light. She nodded and smiled. 'You'll do.'

'This?' Lorak pointed at the brassbound chest that Anria and Haram had struggled to lift onto the base of the wagon.

'Yes,' Haram said.

'Is it fragile?'

'Not really.'

'Good.' Lorak swept it off the base of the wagon with one hand. It thudded onto the floor.

'It is, however, rather explosive,' Haram said.

'But not fragile?'

'No.'

'I'll be more careful then.'

'It might be wise.'

Haram and Lorak grinned at each other.

'Men.' Quila snorted. 'Come on, Anria, Terin is down below. She says you are bright, quick and clever; not that that would be difficult compared to these buffoons.'

'Oh, my love.' Lorak tried to pout.

'You look like you're trying to work out which finger to stick into which nostril and where you put it last.'

Haram opened his mouth to speak.

'Not one word,' Quila warned.

****

Medina enjoyed watching Zarak rage; he always provided such a grand show. The messenger hurried away with orders to begin a citywide search. He was wise to hurry, because Zarak killed three servants with blades of energy lashing from his hotly glowing armour.

'A Shonri killed a squad of Kirruk,' Calderan said. 'When?'

'Are they sure it was a Shonri?' Sora asked. She squealed as she barely avoided the lash of Zarak's anger. The blade of light neatly bisected her chair before flashing onwards into the glowering wall of the chamber, which absorbed the energy as if it were sunlight.

Calderan leapt to his feet. 'Have a care, Zarak.'

Medina could smell the flame building in the Fire-mage's head.

'You dare to threaten me in my own keep?' Zarak glared at Calderan. Who glared back and began to breathe heavily, drawing his mind inward, preparing his most powerful magic.

All show, of course.

'Calm down, both of you,' Rin snapped.

Calderan dropped his gaze from Zarak and sat back in his chair.

Zarak snarled and stalked away from the basalt slab for a moment, before returning to his seat. Sora sat on another chair and watched Zarak with careful eyes.

Delightful, Medina thought, and took the time to cast a few more stones into the water. 'I assume there was only Kirruk blood at the scene? That they were killed up close, with blades, not magic?'

'You assume correctly,' Zarak said.

'Sounds like a Shonri to me.' Medina nodded. 'How close?'

'What?' Zarak slumped down in his seat, his hands flat on the basalt slab, as if he drew solace from its touch; in truth, he drew more than that from the stone.

'How close did the Shonri get? What kind of wounds? What kind of blades?'

'Very close. Short blades. Curved, they think.'

'Sounds like Soldat,' Medina said happily.

'Soldat.' Calderan gulped.

****

'You want to do what?' Haram demanded.

'If I destroy the main switching channel,' Soldat said, 'then their forces will be drawn very thin. That will give you time to get inside the Pyramid, find this map, and destroy it.'

'Destroy the switching channel,' Anria said. 'But… the lights would fail. The city plunged into darkness. Only torches to hold back… Do you *know* what lives beneath this city? What would be released?'

'Yes,' Soldat said.

'But lives is not exactly the right word,' Quila said.

Chapter Fourteen

A LESSER MAGE BROUGHT THE MAP SCROLL from Zarak's treasury and directed two slaves as they carried a large wooden table into the glowering chamber.

'There's no need of another table.' Medina gestured at the basalt slab. 'We could always place the map on that.'

'I think not,' said Zarak.

'Spoilsport.' Medina pointed at a spot very close to the basalt. 'Place the table there.'

'There.' Zarak pointed at a spot much closer to the walls.

'You're no fun.' Medina pouted to hide the fact she checked angles and distances with a calculating gaze. 'A bit further away from the walls,' she said, the simpering quality gone from her voice. 'The walls will absorb too much of the magic. They might even upset the map's fluidity and destroy its effectiveness.' She was all business now; Zarak appreciated that and it gave her leeway to place the table precisely where she needed it to be.

The glowering walls and the basalt slab worked as a single design. The walls absorbed energy and fed it to the slab whence Zarak extracted the power for his most awesome spell-craft.

Medina wanted to know what the basalt did, what function it served in Zarak's power grid, how it worked. Gathering information is always the first stage to theft and she'd never get a better opportunity.

Zarak allowed her to place the table precisely on one of the lines of force between the basalt and the walls—invisible lines that she could detect by the distortion in the air above them, a distortion that none of these vaunted Magi could even sense. They were as blind to magic's true nature as bats were blind to light.

'Oh, Patran!' Medina called.

Calderan's eyes narrowed in anger. 'That's my lesser Mage.'

'Oh,' Medina said. 'Don't you call them apprentices anymore? So hard on their self-esteem to be called lesser. Ah, there you are, sweetheart.' Medina smiled at Patran who had interrupted her awakening and therefore still suffered her displeasure. 'Pick up the strongbox, there's a good lad, and place it on the table.'

Patran hissed as he touched the spell-protected box, but he lifted and carried it to the table, his face a grimace of pain.

Calderan snarled. 'I thought you immune to her.'

'More are immune to me than are not,' Medina said. 'For the dead always outnumber the living. Oh, don't fret, Caldie, it's nothing. Just a little spell cast on his manhood. He didn't even have to touch my flesh, did you sweetheart?'

'I will kill you for this.' Patran set down the strongbox.

Medina blew him a kiss, releasing the thread between them. 'You may go now. Remember your manners in future.'

Rin shuffled on aged legs to the table. Zarak stalked to the table with the stride of a warrior, or rather, what he thought was the stride of a warrior: strong, martial and solid. True warriors had more flex in their step, always ready to move into defence or attack at an instant's notice. Calderan offered Sora his arm but she ignored him and strolled to the table without a backward glance. Calderan scurried after her.

Medina grinned at them all. She adjusted the position of the map, under the guise of removing the brass weights used to hold down its edges. 'Brass is not a good metal to use on such a thing as this.'

'Why?' Rin asked. Stolid, unimaginative Rin; always useful to have around to ask stupid questions.

'Brass affects living tissue. Affects the vibrations of the magic. It won't destroy the map, but the map will need to be recalibrated now.' Medina opened the strongbox, took out four golden pinwheels, and set them spinning at the map's corners.

'What are they?' Zarak asked.

'They draw the essence of the Shonri, of their Scryer marks, back into the map,' Medina lied. In truth, the spell-gold of the pinwheels mapped the forces running through the chamber. The wheels were highly focussed, very delicate, and set by Medina's talented senses and dexterous fingers on the exact edges of a line of force.

'What is that black liquid in those vials?' Sora asked, pointing into the strongbox.

Medina giggled. 'Shonri juice.'

'I beg your pardon?'

'A lock of hair, nail clippings—'

'Sympathetic magic.' Sora sneered. 'How crude.'

'I use what little talent I have.' Medina shrugged. 'I cannot leap from body to body like a mayfly in the throes of passion.' She let Sora see her teeth. 'I cannot focus the power of the elements through my own soul. Ah, fire, such a fickle mistress.' She pouted at Calderan. 'I cannot call forth energy and guide it through crystal, metal, and skin. Or make creatures to carry out my will.' She let her eyes fall downcast before Zarak's imperious gaze. 'I cannot—'

'Careful what you say, Witch,' Rin snapped.

'Oh, Rin, as if I'd insult you.'

'What does the map show?' Zarak asked.

Medina had already seen the lines upon the map, the stains that coiled and twisted, showing the paths of all the Shonri whose essences she had harvested.

'A moment longer,' she said. 'There.' She removed the spinning pinwheels and replaced them with simple stones, before carefully packing the pinwheels away into the strongbox to keep their measurements safe. 'The map shows the paths of the Shonri upon the land, through the sympathetic vibrations,' she smirked at Sora, 'of their scryer marks and souls. It is a very delicate... Oh.' She lifted a hand to her mouth in mock horror. 'Oh, this is not good.'

'What do you see?' Zarak demanded.

'Not good at all.'

'And how do you see it?' Rin leaned forward and peered at the map.

'Oh dear, you will have to act quickly.'

'Act how?' Sora asked.

Medina raised an eyebrow, paused for a moment, let the tension grow, and said. 'Payment in advance.'

'What?' Calderan yelled.

'Payment in advance.'

'The spell-gold is here,' Zarak said. 'We have all brought our share.'

'No.' Medina pointed at the floor beside her. 'The spell-gold isn't here. It may well be close by, but it isn't *here.'*

'This is outrageous,' Calderan said.

'Yes, I suppose it is.' Medina sighed. 'Oh, very well, a little taste of what the map shows.'

'Yes?' Rin asked.

'Soldat isn't alone.'

****

'You can't go alone, Soldat,' Birsin said. He leaned back in an overstuffed leather couch pushed against a wall of the large underground chamber. Turmerix-farmed algae lightpatches provided illumination without the need for magical energy. 'You can't hush your mind enough. They'll have Inoxit loose in the city hunting for you by now.'

Inoxit. The thrill of revenge coursed through Anria even as she stood in the doorway, unsure of where to go, where to sit, what to do. The Seven let their Scryer-marks show in all their glory within the protection of the underground chamber. Anria knew what granted that protection. She recognised the carvings on the stones and shivered. This room was an antechamber to the catacombs.

Did they know what lay there? They said they did, but had they ever looked?

Every line of electrum coiling through the skin of the others showed what they were in comparison to Anria. Her own marks coiled around her body, around her muscles and nerve cells, but they were narrow, tightly prescribed lines, the lines of youth.

Soldat's lines branched again and again, every single muscle and sinew etched in electrum; the marks of a warrior.

'Inoxit?' Quila sat by the kitchen counter picking at some delicately spiced sweetmeats. Her Scryer-marks had speckles of gold in them, of other metals. The electrum, the alloy created by the Machine to make the Shonri what they were, had separated, differentiated under the effect of Quila's magical exertions.

'Rin's here.' Birsin drained his glass tankard of ale. 'She brought six talons with her.' His marks were subtle, ever shifting, flickering into visibility and then disappearing again, the marks of a spy who could hide what he was at will.

'That's seventy-two of the little buggers scuttling around.' Haram sipped at a glass of wine. There were subtle differences between his marks and Soldat's, because Haram wasn't just a warrior. He was also a craftsman, a maker of things, a deeper thinker, and Anria's teacher. 'Birsin's right, Soldat, you won't even reach the switching station.'

'I expected this.' Soldat squatted against the wall, flexing his shoulders and twisting his neck. Scryer-marks popped and bulged within his skin as he exercised. 'Quila will come with me to dampen the emanations of my mind. The rest of you will carry out the main attack.'

'Quila will be needed to breach the defences of the Pyramid,' Birsin said. He lifted his mug for Lorak to refill from the keg under his arm.

Lorak's Scryer-marks spread across his mighty muscles and coated them in silver; his face flat planes of darkness, etched in silver luminescence. He turned his head to glance at Anria and silver flared around his eyes, brighter than she had ever seen Scryer-marks flare before—almost pure gold. The glow faded and he grinned at her, flickers of silver and gold around his mouth.

Birsin took a long swallow of cold ale and said, 'The entry point I've chosen requires magic to unlock it. We'll need Quila.'

'I'll go with Soldat.' Felice lounged back on Birsin's bed. The lines within her skin spread like a tracery of silver lace, like a spider's web, connecting every part of her to every other part and allowing her to connect all whom she soul-touched into one conduit, one mind. 'I can draw his mind into mine and hold it hushed.'

Soldat shuddered. 'I hate that.'

'It's your plan,' Haram said.

Lorak dumped the huge keg of ale upon the ground. 'And now the circumstances have changed. We need Quila with us.' He bounced into the air, punching two holes into the ceiling with his fists. He would have looked like a happy child, were it not for the size of him and the rock dust cascading around his shoulders. 'It's the mark of a true general to be able to change the details of their strategy in the light of new information.' He held out his hands, whitened by rock dust, like a declaiming poet. 'No matter how uncomfortable such a change might be.' He bowed to Soldat.

'You enjoy this too much,' Terin said from the shadows close to the walls. She stood quiet, still, her Scryer-marks tiny, almost invisible, until she moved, when they flared into sudden brightness and blurred with acceleration. She glanced at Anria, slipped down onto another couch with uncommon grace—even for a Shonri—and patted the seat beside her. 'Sit, sister. The ox will want to dance with you if you stay on your feet much longer.'

'It's not often we are all together like this,' Haram said. 'Lorak can get a tad over-exuberant.'

Soldat scowled at the rough stone floor. 'I hate the merge. It feels like being human again.'

'That's the point,' Felice said. 'It hides what you really are.' She studied Anria for a moment. 'You'll come with us too, Anria. We'll need your protection when we move. My senses will be dulled by the merging.'

'Why me? Why can't I take part in the main attack?' Anria asked.

'It's nothing to do with worth, sister,' Terin said.

'You were born in this city,' Felice said. 'You know its streets. That may well prove vital.'

Soldat lifted his head. 'Two attacks, at the switching station and the Pyramid. It is agreed then?'

'It is agreed,' the others answered in one voice, then looked at Anria.

'What?'

'You're family now,' Lorak said. 'You get a vote.'

'And if I vote no?'

'Then we argue until the vote is unanimous,' Haram said. 'This is old Shonri business. Family. We all agree or none act.'

'It's why we tend to hunt alone most of the time.' Lorak winked.

'Not always alone.' Quila stuck her tongue out at him.

'We're the exception, my love,' Lorak said. 'I just do as you say and thus we are always of one voice.'

'If only.' Quila sighed. 'We have to agree, sister,' she said to Anria. 'Which is why Soldat bounced us into his plan by acting first.'

'Like he's never done that before.' Birsin sniffed and sipped at his ale.

'How do you vote, sister?' Felice asked.

'You're the Old Ones,' Anria blurted. 'I agree with you, obviously.'

'It is agreed,' Terin said. She glanced at Anria. 'We're not our legends, sister. We're not infallible. Your voice is needed for more than just sycophantic assent.'

Anria flushed, her small, narrow Scryer-marks bright within her skin.

'Give her time.' Lorak winked at her again. 'She'll realise we're all idiots soon enough.' He clapped his huge hands together. 'Right, Haram, what's in the box?'

Haram opened his mouth to answer but Birsin spoke first. 'Rin also brought ten fighting pairs of Callorts.' Birsin ticked off the enemy forces on his fingertips. 'Calderan brought another eight. Zarak has an entire regiment of Kirruk, that's a thousand of the nasty pieces of lizard turd.'

'Less six.' Soldat rose from his position by the wall and poured himself a mug of ale, waving away Lorak and lifting the keg with both arms and a grunt of effort.

'Oh, sorry,' Birsin said. 'One thousand Kirruk, less the six Soldat butchered. Plus Zarak's Raptors. This new Lamia has a small force of human mercenaries, well armed, but they're only human. Oh, and Zarak has Callort guards on every gate into the Pyramid, so that's another ten fighting pairs.'

'So, fifty-six Callorts, seventy-two Inoxit, one thousand Kirruk—less six—a few humans and a whole bunch of bloody huge eagles to fight.' Lorak rubbed his hands together. 'This is going to be fun.'

Quila wiped her hand over her face. 'Somebody stop him talking, please. There are also the lesser Magi, the servants, the slaves, and the other creatures to consider.'

'Plus,' Haram said, 'Calderan's a Fire-mage, Zarak's armour has forceshield weapons, and Rin has survived at least four Shonri attacks in the last decade.'

'Yes, yes.' Lorak nodded. 'That's why Soldat planned so carefully.'

Birsin snorted.

'We've fought worse,' Terin said. 'We've fought our own kind and won.'

Silence.

Anria looked around the room; each of her new comrades stared at a spot where they could see no other's gaze. Their Scryer-marks hushed, quiet; even Soldat's faded away to almost nothing.

Felice spoke into the silence. 'We did what had to be done.'

Nods around the room. Glasses raised in tribute. 'To the fallen.' Glasses drained and thrown against the walls to shatter into fragments.

'You could've all picked the same damn spot,' Birsin complained, gazing at the glass scattered across the floor.

'You don't have a fireplace,' Haram pointed out.

'Do you really think you'll be coming back here after this?' Soldat asked.

'Now.' Lorak grabbed Quila and lifted her. She squealed. He dropped onto the sofa beside Terin and Anria, with Quila ensconced in his lap. 'What's in the box, Haram?'

****

'What do you mean the spell-gold is not here?' Zarak demanded.

'It's on its way,' Calderan said. 'Coming in by Manta. It should be here in a few days.'

'A few days.' Rin slapped her hand on the wooden table, careful not to touch the map; Magi were inclined to be superstitious about sympathetic magic. Medina sneered in her mind, but kept her face blandly smiling.

Sora said, 'That's too long.'

It looked like Calderan had lost another lover. So sad. Medina stretched. Calderan couldn't help but look. Sora's cheeks tightened in outrage. Oh yes, Calderan had definitely lost another lover.

'I can wait,' Medina said in her most innocent voice.

'Wait?' Zarak thundered. 'Soldat is running around my city with a band of Shonri pups and you expect us to wait?'

Medina didn't think it was quite the time to explain that Soldat wasn't exactly bringing young Shonri into the city on a training mission. If she let the Magi know that all the Seven were in the city, they might panic. If they panicked, they might forget to pay her.

That would never do.

She glanced at the map. No movement. They were still hidden away from the map by the spell-craft of the catacombs, but they could hardly be advancing through there. She'd see them when they returned to the surface. Safe enough to play for a while.

'Perhaps one of you could loan Calderan the money,' Medina mused aloud, as if the thought had just occurred to her. 'It's only a few bars of spell-gold, after all.'

'Loan,' Rin spluttered. 'Trust… him?'

'Ah yes, I do see your point.' Medina nodded, allowing her hair to fall across her face and hide her grin.

'I'm good for it,' Calderan protested.

'I don't want to go to war over a few bars of spell-gold,' Zarak said.

'Go to war?' Sora asked.

'When he doesn't pay me back,' Zarak growled.

'I'm good for it.'

'I have extra in my baggage,' Rin said. 'Enough to cover a third of Calderan's share.'

'Wait.'

'I can cover a third from my treasury vaults easily enough,' Zarak said.

'Now hold on a minute.' Calderan's eyes pleaded with Sora.

She smiled sweetly. 'I can cover another third.'

'I'm good for it,' Calderan whined.

'You should have brought it with you,' Zarak said. 'They did.'

'I negotiated for this map. It was my idea.'

'Then you should have asked for the key,' Rin said. 'You're out, Calderan. Please leave before we have any unpleasantness.'

'Go now,' Zarak ordered. He was always so impressively arrogant.

'You don't have the power to force me out. I can bring this Pyramid down around your ears.'

'Don't be foolish,' Sora said.

Calderan's face flushed scarlet, a dangerous sign in a Fire-mage. 'How will you get back with only a few human mercenaries to protect you?'

'I'm a Lamia, dear.' Sora studied her fingernails. 'You protect me only from the inconvenience of finding a new body.'

'They killed Cinome!' Calderan cried.

Even Medina winced. No Lamia wished to be reminded of Cinome's disappearance.

Sora's voice became ice cold. 'Leave now or else I will reach into your head and turn your mind into broken splinters of memory. I'll take particular pleasure in twisting the delights of my flesh into fragments of nightmare that you will see whenever you close your eyes.'

Medina was warming to Sora.

'Unravel my mind and you unleash my power,' Calderan said, triumphant. 'If I lose control, all will burn.'

'So?' Sora asked. 'Your point being?'

'I thought you loved me.'

'This body has needs. I may have to change for one less perverted.'

Medina laughed aloud. She shouldn't have, but she really couldn't help it.

'Bitch,' Calderan snarled.

'Correct,' Medina replied. 'The door is that way.'

The heat rose from Calderan in waves, shimmering in the air above his head. None of the other Magi noticed. Even Sora looked on without a trace of concern. They were utterly blind to the dangerous instability at the heart of Calderan.

But he was nothing if not a coward.

He swallowed his anger, swallowed back the heat, held it tight within his stomach and strode from the room.

'Now that's settled,' Rin said. 'What does the map show?'

Medina glanced at the floor beside her. 'I don't see a sack of spell-gold.'

'Oh, really.' Rin threw up her hands in disgust.

'Yes,' Medina said. 'Really.' She glanced at the map. The Shonri had not moved. Still plenty of time.

CHAPTER FIFTEEN

SOLDAT SAID, 'IT DOES WHAT?'

'It creates dead zones.' Haram repeated the phrase with obvious relish.

The brass-bound trunk lay open on the floor between them, stuffed full of metal tubes and strange wires. At its very centre lay a fist-sized sphere of some dull grey metal.

'How?' Anria reached out to touch the sphere.

'Don't do that,' Haram snapped. 'That's a stasis sphere. Your Scryer-marks might breach it.'

'I threw that off the wagon,' Lorak said.

'Yes. It's not fragile.' Haram grinned. 'Well, not very.'

'You knew I'd sweep it off the wagon.'

'I knew, but it really isn't dangerous until it's armed.'

'Good to know.' Lorak kicked the trunk.

'What the hell are you doing?' Haram snapped.

'Testing it. If I have to carry it into the Pyramid, I need to know how much punishment it can take when it's strapped to my back.'

'Good point,' Haram said.

'How does it work?' Anria was beginning to worry whether Lorak and Haram should be within a hundred miles of each other, let alone in the same room.

'Inside the sphere there's a plasma of spell-gold, Scryer's silver, platinum, copper, and some other trace elements.'

'Shonri electrum,' Quila said.

'Yes. There's also some dragon bone mixed in there too. It took the Turmerix a while to find the right mix for maximum effect.'

'They tested it?' Anria asked.

'No, they...' Haram paused. 'They think about it. Hard to explain.

They took the idea from my mind. I felt the breadth of their hive, so many pathways, all working on the problem, all testing it by pure imagination.' He shook his head. 'They lost me soon enough. It was like watching ripples on the sea turning into one mighty wave. The wave is the correct mix. It took them months of thinking to work it all out. I only linked for a few minutes. Took me three weeks to recover.'

'I felt the jolt,' Felice said. 'From the other side of the continent.'

'So that's where you disappeared to when we were training to attack Cinome,' Anria said.

'Yes.'

'How hot will it burn?' Soldat asked.

'I wouldn't want to be within a mile of it. Though the Pyramid will absorb most of the blast, of course. If we set it in the exact centre of the Pyramid, after we get the map, then it shouldn't extend beyond the boundaries of its gardens. Mostly. Maybe a quarter mile?'

'The city,' Anria said.

'What about it?'

'There are people here, innocent people.'

'Nobody is innocent,' Birsin said.

'Some are.' Anria looked around at the legendary Shonri surrounding the electrum bomb. 'You told me I am one of you now, with a full vote. Come with me. All of you. Let me show you what you wish to unleash.'

Soldat said, 'We know—'

'Have you ever seen it?' Anria stormed through the door marked with the carvings she remembered so well.

She knew the catacombs. Exploring them was a childhood prank for the rich and powerful in the city, a shuddering, delightful breach of the rules. However, they always made sure to take protection with them, in the shape of a few slaves to feed to the darkness if it got too close. Anria shivered, remembering Korat. He'd been right to despise her.

The others followed her through the doorway. She wasn't sure that they would but they did and pride held her in its grip for a moment—but only for a moment, because then she led them down the stairs.

Cold, hissing darkness below. Anria let her eyes adjust, let her Scryer-marks bathe everything in greenish light. The last time she walked down into the catacombs below the city, she and her giggling friends had carried torches. They were not giggling when they left.

The eight Shonri stepped out onto a balcony cut into the rock, a long balustrade in front of them, ancient curved supports holding up a solid piece of finely worked stone. Glints of metal flashed here and there, some gemstones, but not many, most taken as trophies by empty-headed children like Anria—the children of the wealthy.

A sense of space expanded around them; a high vaulted ceiling above, dark depths below.

Anria looked over the edge of the balustrade, down to where the bone piles lay. There were no graveyards in the City of Lights. The rich were interred in mausoleums above ground, but the corpses of the poor were brought here, underground, to the quarries where the very stone of their city was excavated.

The people of the city had been too greedy for stone and dug too deep. The magic unleashed below the city energised the souls of the dead, held them tight within its grasp. Only light kept them away from the living. The Scryer-marks of the Shonri fulfilled the same function for their bearers.

A seething mass of dark shadows writhed below, not a hint of green—the colour of life—in the Scryer-sight of the Shonri. The shadows lapped against the walls of stone, crawling upwards only to fall back as if too weak to hold on, to gain purchase on the pockmarked walls. Daylight still ruled above and the spirits of the dead could feel the weak sunlight of a winter's sun, even through the yards of solid ground between them and the surface.

'That is what you wish to unleash with your plan, Soldat.' Anria pointed at the fog of trapped souls below. A fog that parted, stretched up towards the sound of her voice, and then fell back, exhausted by the effort. 'This is what the lights of this city hold back in the night and now you,' she glared at Haram, 'want to destroy the only hope there is of stopping this *darkness*, this *soul-filled dread*, this *Terror*.' She'd learned those names for the trapped spirits a long time ago. The shadows seemed to cringe at the sound of them.

'This is power, Anria,' Quila said. 'Can't you feel it? This is what makes Zarak so dominant. This is what allows him to control such mighty creatures as the Raptors.'

A flash of gold around Lorak's eyes at the sound of Zarak's name, a flash that disappeared almost as soon as Anria spotted it.

She turned and led them back up the stairs, back up to Birsin's lair, leaving the dead behind. The others waited for her to speak when she stood over the open box of Haram's electrum bomb.

'We must give the people of this city a chance to escape,' she said.

'How?' Soldat asked.

'When did you intend to destroy the switching station?'

Soldat shrugged. 'At dusk, of course. Maximum panic. Without the station, the lights will fail. We go in, find the map, get out, leave this bomb behind as a parting gift.' He grinned savagely.

'And I would have agreed," Anria said. "We all know how dangerous the map is, but now Haram intends to destroy the Pyramid itself. To create a dead zone, to let the *darkness* out, and I don't agree anymore.' Anria gestured to the stone above her. 'There are alternate paths for the magic to flow from the Pyramid to the lights. They take time to energise, but they would save the city. They would keep the lights burning. You mean to take away even that hope. The people have to be given time to escape. We have to do that much for them.'

Lorak said, 'I told you she'd figure it out.' But Anria remembered that flash of gold around his eyes, that look of utter hatred on his face, at the sound of Zarak's name.

'What's your plan?' Felice asked.

'We destroy the switching station now. It's nearly noon. That will give the people five hours to escape before night falls. They must have a chance to flee.'

'That'll increase the risk,' Soldat said. 'Our gifts make us more effective night fighters.'

'Who cares? Let them all die,' Birsin snarled. 'There are no innocents in this city.'

'There are over a million people in this city,' Anria said. 'What's the point of saving the world if there is nobody left to live in freedom?'

****

Zarak laid his hands on the basalt slab. The pain of millions of souls trapped in the bone pits beneath the city pulsed into him, through him, and into the walls of the chamber. He stood in the centre of their lines of force, his body gaining youth, his armour gaining power, and his mind pushing through the transcendental barrier into the minds of the Raptors.

His Raptors.

Bred from eagles, solitary creatures that pair-mated but didn't live in flocks. Zarak had changed their brain structure to allow them to congregate, changed their very consciousness, connected them into one group—an interconnected flock, his eyes over his city. However, the more Raptor minds that co-mingled in his flock, the harder they were to control, to command. They grew resistant to his mental instructions. Zarak knew that the flock needed culling; a winnowing of the weak. But the almost too-large flock would be useful in the hunt for the Shonri.

The souls trapped in limbo below, in the creeping darkness under the city, screeched in Zarak's mind. Captured by the matrix within the basalt, they were held tight and forced to surrender part of their life force, their essence, to his demands. The basalt slab, large, oblong, heavy, ripped from the rock by men who dug too deep. This very room, this very Pyramid, designed to funnel, to moderate, to channel the power of that matrix.

Taking the matrix and making it work for him was Zarak's greatest achievement. A few million screaming souls were nothing compared to that power.

He used the energetic residue of death to lance his way into the conjoined minds of his Raptor flock. The Raptors wheeled through the sky to carry out his specific, but complex commands.

Medina held her face still, smiling within herself. She listened to Zarak's mind, tasted the connection between him and the basalt, through the basalt to the screaming dead, and then up into his magnificent flock of Raptors. The need to know how the basalt actually worked almost drove her to drink too deep, to taste too much; even lust hadn't uncovered such deep knowledge.

Almost, but not quite. Reaching for that knowledge now would warn the powerful Mage of her presence in his mind. She couldn't hope to stand against him, not here, not in his own keep, not in full view.

But still.

She knew what to look for now. Watching him, slipping into his mind as he instructed his Raptors, gave her the beginnings of an understanding, showed her the shape of the matrix, allowed her to discard possibilities; but it hadn't yet shown her the mechanism.

The readings from the pinwheels would show her more. Allow her to start to reconstruct the spell-craft needed to purloin this power.

She was glad she had come here now. This was so very, very instructive.

If only Rin would stop clouding the aether with her exhaustive micromanaging instructions to her minions. If only Sora would stop sending testing tendrils of energy against Medina's tightly closed defences. If only the Shonri had not learned about the map.

But then, without the Shonri, she wouldn't be here now, at the heart of Zarak's power, learning its secrets.

Sadly, she withdrew from Zarak's mind lest he catch her. She had learned all that she could for now. A quick glance down at the map. Some of the Shonri moved towards the Pyramid, but Soldat and Felice still hid away in their underground den. Until they moved, the attack wouldn't be imminent.

She could see the paths of the Seven upon this land, where they congregated, where the paths clustered in only a few spots; places the Magi could attack in the hope of finding the Machine.

Not her concern. The Shonri would adapt. They were remarkably hard to kill.

When Felice and Soldat moved, she'd have to act quickly, but until that moment she could wait and gain more insight into the workings of the basalt matrix.

Anyway, her payment had not yet arrived.

Chapter Sixteen

THE RAPTORS FLEW LAZY SPIRALS above the streets of the city, looking down upon the thronging mass of humans below. Their hunger sated, the Raptors searched for anything out of the ordinary, their interdependent minds guided by the instructions of their master.

On the streets of the city, people haggled, argued, lived in the daylight. They never looked up, never gazed at the clouds, at the sky, because to look up would be to see the Raptors, and to remember their place in all of this—insignificant and enslaved humans for whom even death was not a release from bondage.

Better not to think too hard about what flew above their heads, or about what lay beneath their feet. Better to live in the light and never look into the dark. Better not to see, not to think, not to act.

Three cloaked figures pushed their way through the crowds, unnoticed by Raptor and human alike.

Soldat puffed and wiped the sweat from his forehead. Even in the cold of a winter's day, he sweated in his cloak. No Scryer-marks showed on his face, on his skin; he could have walked through the crowd with his face exposed and nobody would have known he was anything other than human.

Human.

A victim.

A slave.

The merging of his mind into the nestled pebble of Felice's spirit thrust him back into memory. He snarled into the air.

A Raptor swooped in for a closer look, peering into the margins of the ambient magic. However, Felice didn't use magic to obscure Soldat's Scryer-marks; she enveloped them in her own soul. Therefore, the

Raptor perceived nothing, wheeled away, and continued its search.

Soldat was loaded down with weapons, the weight of which he would barely have noticed if his Scryer-marks flared: a repeating crossbow, with numerous magazines; a heavy crossbow, with heavier bolts in a quiver on his hip; a backpack full of explosives constructed by crafty Haram to destroy the switching station. Haram had brought all the materials with him in the wagon and quickly built the explosives after interrogating Birsin about the layout of the switching station. He hadn't guaranteed the effect, but he grinned happily when handing Soldat the backpack. He knew Soldat's methods.

Soldat's personal weapons—the scythes, the flexible saw, the knives, the tools of a gardener transformed into implements of bloody death—lay upon his belt as they always did, but it was all so heavy, so ridiculously heavy, for a mere human. Soldat sucked more air into his lungs and took another step forward.

They left the safety of Birsin's den at the same time as the others, heading away from their comrades to carry out their part of the plan. A plan agreed in the old way. Felice hid Soldat's mind within her own, but the merge was hard on them both.

His memories crawled through her mind. Jani laughed again within Felice. She could hear Jani's voice, smell her scent, taste her breath. The happy laughter of children on the breeze, squabbling, playing, then, finally, weeping as the plague swept away their lives.

A Mage-birthed plague. Soldat's rage a huge thing, solid, unyielding, ruthless. He wouldn't stop until the last Mage fell, or until he fell, and he didn't much care which came first. To Soldat the fight was all. Laughter lost on the wind, love dying on discoloured sheets, happiness putrefying on the bone. All that he was buried under the loam on his fingers from digging too many graves.

Felice was still Shonri, still stronger, faster, more robust than human, even when merged with Soldat's mind—but her senses, the senses she relied upon more than she wished to admit, became hazed, dazed, distracted by the maze of Soldat's mind resting within her own.

And so they relied on Anria to guide them.

Anria's gaze flickered across the thronging crowds from within the shadow of her hood. There were faces in the throng she had known since childhood, older now, wrinkled, drawn thin by the stress of living so closely under the boot heel of the Magi.

Would they recognise her as she recognised them? Would they see beyond the electrum coiling within her skin to the soul beneath? She saw beneath the cruelty and the malice, the seething distrust, the raging fear, to the truth of their lives. They were humans, brutalised, victimised, enslaved humans, but humans still. They still loved, they still hoped, they still dreamed that one day all this would pass and freedom would be theirs. Anria knew this, for she had once been such as they and her dreams had never died.

Inoxit, a full talon of the creatures, scuttled across the ground, their white exoskeletons glistening in the sunlight. Dangerous creatures, bred to hunt Shonri. Anria jerked at a sudden realisation: these Inoxit were larger than the ones she had fought before. Their compound eyes glittered brighter colours, their jaws longer with more points upon the mandibles. Anria noted their slightly slower movement as they came close, in an instinctive search pattern, though the human crowds. People shrank back from their fearsome appearance.

Anria kept her mind hushed, not allowing even a hint of her Scryer-marks to flare. Her last, her only contact with the Inoxit had taught her an important lesson. She wasn't as fast as Terin, as strong as Lorak, as skilled as Soldat. She didn't have the magic of Quila, the guile of Birsin, the craft of Haram. And she couldn't move within the shadow of a thought like Felice.

Her weapons changed that bloody day and Haram had helped her design new versions for the fight. The disc she carried on her left hip irised open into a thin but incredibly strong shield—with an edge so sharp it was a weapon in its own right. On the same hip, in a scabbard set for a draw across the belly, rode her sword, strong, light, with edges so sharp they could shear through the exoskeleton of an Inoxit. The tapered triangular blade would pierce the hide of a Callort if driven with enough force. The hand-and-a-half hilt allowed her to bring that force to bear.

Spring bows, strapped to her forearms as part of her vambraces, gave her ranged attack and defence in a single Haram-built device. Smaller blades held in sheaths scattered across her body completed her arsenal.

With the addition of the crossbows and bolts that Haram supplied for this mission, she was as heavily armed as any of the others, but still her skin crawled as the Inoxit scuttled close.

She remembered Korat and itched to let her Scryer-marks shine, to throw back her hood, to make them pay for what their kindred had done.

'Quiet now.' Felice sent a needle-sharp thought into Anria's mind. A tightly controlled thought to avoid detection. *'Keep your mind hushed.'*

****

What was that? Medina stared hard at the map. A flash of something. Gone now. No mark left upon the map, as if it never existed.

Why were Birsin and the five other Shonri clustered there? Beneath the very walls of the Pyramid? There was no way in through there.

Where was her payment?

****

'So that's why you wanted us to waterproof our weapons,' Haram said, gazing down into the pool.

The Shonri crouched under the cover of a hedge in the ornamental gardens that surrounded the Pyramid. A low wall protected their rear. Before them lay the edge of a manmade lake that flowed under the walls of the Pyramid. An observation bridge spanned the pool at its narrowest point, hard up against the Pyramid wall rearing above. The roar of the weir in the background would deafen a human, but none of the Shonri saw the need to raise their voices.

'That's a Manta pool,' Terin said.

'Yes.' Birsin kept a constant watch above. He knew the paths of the Raptors better than most.

The weir fed water into the pool from the river beyond. The Manta-spawn couldn't surmount this weir, but river fish could swim over it and into the pool. The immature Mantas devoured any fish that entered their domain. In the ocean, Manta rays gave birth to live young, young large enough to defend themselves, but Manta-ship young were born from incubated eggs, were much smaller than their natural cousins, and a great deal more vicious.

'How old?' Lorak asked.

'They ain't turned cannibal yet,' Birsin replied.

Manta-spawn were transmuted, ferocious little creatures, bred by the thousands, grown in pools that trickle-fed magic into them as they matured and grew and fed. Fed on meat. Any meat, it didn't matter if it was dead and stinking or alive and screaming, so long as there was enough of it; it took a great deal of protein to grow a Manta-ship.

When the spawn grew too big for the pool to hold them comfortably, their skin colour turned from a mottled brown to a clear white and a frenzy of cannibalism began. A frenzy that continued until only a single, huge Manta-spawn remained. The creature was then taken from the water, bloated even further by the direct application of esoteric magic, its skin blackened by it, until it grew large enough to fly through the streams of magic encircling the Earth, with a cabin full of wealthy passengers welded to its broad back.

'So, hundreds of the snappy little buggers,' Quila said. 'Feeding on anything thrown into the water.'

'With sting-spikes in their tails,' Haram added.

'It's the only undefended entrance,' Birsin said.

'With good bloody reason,' Haram snapped.

'And you want me to…?' Quila asked.

'Quiet them down a bit so we can swim through,' Birsin said.

'There'll be a grill beyond there.' Haram pointed at the water flowing under the Pyramid. 'To stop them escaping into the river downstream of the Pyramid.'

'Not a grill,' Birsin said. 'There's another smaller pool inside. It's where the magic is trickled in. There's a forcewall further on.'

'Forcewall,' Terin yelped. 'Like a wall of energy designed to make living flesh into unliving flesh?'

'Yes. Manta-ships are immune to damage from a forcewall, so any spawn that come into contact with it and die are not true Mantas. It's a culling mechanism. They can't pass through the forcewall, but—'

'That's quite a strong current.' Haram studied the water.

'The pipes get a bit narrow.'

'Narrow?' Lorak flexed his huge muscles.

'You should be able to get through, but you may have to trail the box behind.'

'The bomb, you mean.' Haram smiled without mirth. 'The bomb built around a sphere filled with ravening, magic-eating plasma.'

Quila raised her hand, for all the world like a pupil asking for permission to speak. 'You really ought to know something.'

'What?' Birsin asked.

'Uh-oh,' Lorak said.

Quila scratched at her ear. 'I can't quiet them.'

CHAPTER SEVENTEEN

MEDINA COUNTED THE SPELL-GOLD three times. She knew she ought to hurry, but the looks of barely suppressed impatience on the faces of the three Magi were just too delicious to pass up.

'Forty-eight bars,' she said for the third time, then she smiled and leaned back in her chair. 'All there, though…' she rubbed at the bridge of her nose '…I'm only a poor little Witch, with only the dregs of sympathetic magic at my disposal. Maybe I made a mistake. Maybe…'

'It's all there!' Zarak roared.

'…I should get a second opinion.'

'From who?' Sora asked.

'Oh, Gilbert,' Medina called.

From the shadows of the glowering walls a darker patch of shadow moved. A shadow that faded away to reveal the scrawny form of a Gilbon-tracker.

'That's one of Calderan's Gilbons,' Rin said.

Zarak raised an arm, aiming his force armour at the creature.

Gilbert faded back into the gloom.

'Damn it,' Zarak snarled. His gaze darted wildly around the room, trying to see the creature, but Gilbert's native talents, enhanced by Medina's skills, made him impossible to find, even for a Mage as powerful as Zarak.

'Gilbert did belong to Calderan,' Medina said, 'but then Calderan set him to track me.' She let her smile broaden to show her finely shaped teeth and the coldness in her eyes. 'I ate his soul on a Worm-train and now he belongs to me. Don't you, Gilbert?'

'Yes, mistress.' The whispered words skittered around the room with no obvious place of origin.

'Where is it?' Zarak slapped his hand onto the basalt slab, drawing energy to power his Mage-sight. Rin sent out the call for her own Gilbons, summoning them to the chamber in the hope that they could hunt down the interloper. Sora, ah Sora; the Lamia stood erect and still, her eyes staring at nothing, as she let her spirit twitch out in search. She almost uncovered Gilbert's position at the first attempt.

That would never do.

'Come here, Gilbert,' Medina commanded. 'Pick up the gold, place it in this sack, then wait in the shadows for me.' A calculated risk, because now Sora knew where to look, but Medina said, 'Now, you want to learn how to read the map?'

Sora blinked as her spirit returned to her body. Rin hunched forward. Zarak lowered his arm.

'We want the key,' Rin said.

'Good.' Medina closed up her strongbox, fixed the clasps firmly in place, and re-energised the security spells. 'Look at it and I will show you the secret.'

'We are looking at the map,' Zarak said.

'No, look deeper.' While the three Magi focused on the map, distracted, Medina passed the strongbox to the waiting Gilbert. 'This is a perfect map, made by the purest magic. Every feature is exact, perfect, down to the smallest detail. Look into it. See beyond the surface.'

'It's just squiggles and stains,' Sora complained.

'The stains are the paths of the Shonri Old Ones,' Medina said as Gilbert faded away into a darker patch of shadow. 'Look deeper.'

Surprisingly, it was Rin, good old unimaginative Rin, who broke through the blockage first. 'Oh my,' she breathed. 'I can see it. I can see everything. I can see every street of the city, every hovel, every… what's that? Over there. By the switching station.'

Medina looked. Felice must have merged with Soldat, which changed the signature of both their spirits. Interesting, but it was time to go if they were unmerging. 'That's Soldat and Felice,' she said, 'and there are the rest of the Seven beside the walls of the Pyramid.'

'What?' Zarak roared. 'The Seven! All of them! Here?'

'Yes.' Medina held out her arms and shrugged. 'I can only assume that they learned of the existence of the map.'

'You knew,' Sora said.

'Yes.'

'You knew they were here and you didn't tell us?' Rin snarled.

'You hadn't paid me.' Medina stepped back into Gilbert's shadow and disappeared from the sight and senses of the Magi.

'You bitch!' Sora screamed.

'Correct,' Medina replied with Gilbert's untraceable whisper.

****

'You want to do what?' Birsin asked.

'I can't quiet them,' Quila said, 'but I can make them change. I can make them turn pearl-white. Make them into cannibals. They won't try to eat us, then.'

'They'll go into frenzy, biting at anything that moves,' Haram pointed out. 'And you expect us to swim through that? Holding our breath?'

'They won't bite us,' Quila said. 'They only attack other Manta-spawn when they are white. They only begin eating other meat when there is no spawn left to eat and they turn black when they become Manta-ships.'

'How will they know we're not Manta-spawn?' Birsin asked.

'Wrong size, wrong shape, not as white as the inside of an oyster shell.' Quila scratched her cheek. 'I think there are pheromones involved too.'

'We'll be bathing in their pheromones,' Terin said.

'I never said it was a perfect plan.'

'You know,' Lorak rumbled. 'We may be getting a little sloppy in our old age. This is the most half-arsed plan we have ever come up with.'

'If Lorak think it's a bad idea…' Haram shook his head. 'Whatever. We don't have much choice. It's either this or use the front door.'

'We can do that.' Lorak held up fists encased in cestus gloves. The only weapons he ever carried. Heavy armour protected his body and if he found himself in need of a longer-ranged weapon, there was generally something lying around that he could throw. He liked to keep things simple, did Lorak.

'Do we do this or not?' Quila pointed at the Manta pool just as several of the spawn broke the surface in unison. Their brown bodies, mottled with patches of red, looked like drying blood clots, blood clots with sharp teeth and a disagreeable disposition. The spawn arched through the water and then dived again. 'Do we do this?'

'Yes.' Terin touched the twin hilts of her forceblades.

'Yes.' Haram hefted his axe.

'Yes.' Birsin's weapons were hidden, unusual, and plentiful.

Lorak gazed at the water for a long moment. 'Help me get this bomb off my back.'

'It is agreed?' Quila asked.

'It is agreed,' the others responded.

****

The switching station stood on the top of a hill, a long triangular building which held the main switching channel for the magic flowing from the Pyramid to the lights of the city. Magic that flowed out of a spell-gold pipe over a foot in diameter.

Magic formed in the bone pits beneath the city, transformed from screaming misery in the matrix of the basalt, transferred into the pipe to gush forth into the switching station in a tumbling, foaming cascade of pure magical energy which lashed at the sides of the triangular basin. A basin criss-crossed with catwalks and controlled by sluices, which pumped the magic into smaller channels, which led to still smaller channels, which led to still smaller pipes, which split repeatedly into capillary pipes and distributed the energy to the City of Lights.

To keep the lights blazing and the dead trapped.

In the centre of that gushing magic the energy shone a brilliant white, but foaming particles of red, orange, yellow, green, blue, indigo and violet popped and shimmered within that central core of whiteness, with a broken edge of darkness roiling along the outside of the flow, smashing itself into nothingness against the sides of the basin.

Anria loosed another bolt from the repeating crossbow. 'Run!' she yelled at the workers, at the lesser Magi and technicians. The crossbow held at waist level, one-handed, as her other hand worked the magazine, her aim rock-steady.

'Run!' She killed the Magi but let the technicians flee. 'Run! Get your people out of this city.' Diamond-clay bolts exploded, blasting holes in the walls of the switching station. 'Tonight the soul-filled dread rises unchecked by light.'

She discarded the empty diamond-clay magazine and switched to magnesium bolts. 'Run!' She shot a bolt into the back of a fleeing Mage.

Bright light flared as the bolt caught alight and burned as brightly as the sun for a moment. Anria's Scryer-marks filtered the intense brightness. A technician flung up a hand to protect his eyes, stumbled when a falling lump of masonry struck the catwalk he ran across, and tumbled into the basin of roiling magic. He screamed as the rainbow particles consumed his flesh. A shadow of darkness blossomed in the flow as his soul, trapped by the magic, raged at its death.

Other dark patches in the magic, other souls trapped when humans fell into the flow, their raging souls all that remained of their existence.

'Run!' Anria worked the bolt of the crossbow and fired again.

Felice and Soldat saw none of this. The cost of unmerging their spirits forced them to their knees. Disorientated by the extraction, Soldat couldn't focus, couldn't see, for long moments.

Their entire beings dragged apart, pulled asunder, their memories fighting to find their way back to their rightful homes, reforming, remaking themselves anew. Felice guided the transition. She wanted no part of Soldat to remain within her. His unyielding anger would tear her apart, so she pushed, pulled, chivvied the pieces of his mind back into their proper places.

Soldat let his Scryer-marks flare, let the flame of his strength, his power, his uncompromising personality lash free within his trembling body. Deliberately, he drew the enemy to him, to help Felice in her work and to let Haram and the others enter the Pyramid undetected. He didn't even attempt to control the pulse of magic, his signature. The enemy would converge on this spot, on this location.

If his plan worked.

Felice rose to her feet and focussed on the realm of the mind, the connection. She could sense the others even across the breadth of the continent, the breadth of the world, and she could feel them now, preparing to begin their own battle; but the unmerging disrupted the pattern, disrupted her finely wrought Scryer gifts, and left her unconnected for long moments.

As the Raptors swooped towards the switching station in a mighty flock, as the Inoxit scuttled across the ground on many legs, cutting through any human who stood in their way, climbing up and over houses and sheer hillsides as if they were level ground, as a circle of death and destruction closed in on the tattered stone of the switching station, Anria loaded another magazine of diamond-clay bolts into her crossbow. Her cloak thrown back. Her Scryer-marks ablaze. Standing guard over her family as the enemy advanced towards them.

****

'That's the Manta pool,' Zarak said. 'They can't come through there.'

'Call back your forces,' Sora cried. 'There are five Old Ones about to enter this Pyramid, this keep of yours. Five of the Seven.'

'I thought you didn't care.' Rin laughed, a liquid sound. 'I thought you could just waft away into another body and leave all this behind.'

'Cinome,' Sora spat. 'One of those bastards killed Cinome.'

'Yes, they did, didn't they?' Rin laughed again.

'That bitch Medina.' Zarak raged as he strode towards the basalt.

'Did you expect her to be anything else?' Rin asked. She closed her eyes and opened her mind to her Inoxit, her Callorts, to command them in this battle. 'Call your humans, Sora. They can stand guard in this chamber.' Her breathing settled as she interfaced with her forces. 'We will make our stand here.'

'You can stand wherever you want.' Sora lashed out with her mind, into the open minds of Zarak and Rin, minds opened to command their forces. The blast of pure mental anguish struck like lightning. 'I'm going to be running away.'

Zarak and Rin's creatures staggered under the force of Sora's treacherous mental attack. Raptors spiralled towards the ground until they threw off the power of Sora's blast. Zarak struggled to regain control of them, but Rin managed to hold her Inoxit and Callorts in place. Rin was powerful in her own way and her creatures were tied to her more strongly than Zarak's Raptors. The confusion lasted only seconds, for they were powerful Magi, but the attack gave Sora her chance to flee.

She took the map with her.

CHAPTER EIGHTEEN

'THEY'RE IN POSITION,' FELICE SAID. 'The Manta pool. Brilliant.'

'And crazy.' Soldat knelt on the floor of the switching station, now empty of the enemy, unpacking the explosive and tools.

Felice unsnapped her bow from her belt. She jerked it downwards and then upwards. The arms of the bow snapped out, clicked into place, cams and pulleys rotated to tension the triple strings. Only one string propelled the arrows, the other two simply provided leverage, lowering the strength required to use the bow. This meant, in the hands of a Shonri, that the draw-weight of this bow could drive an arrow through several inches of rock.

Soldat finished arranging the explosives and equipment to his liking and attached them to his belt. He placed his weapon harness on the ground behind him, loaded and ready, awaiting his need.

Felice fitted an arrow to the bowstring and took position behind one of the holes Anria placed in the walls with her diamond-clay barrage, holes that gave protection but also gave a good view of the enemy.

Anria lifted her repeating crossbow. 'Here they come,' she said, as she checked the magazine. 'Set the charges, Soldat.'

Soldat threw himself into the foaming magic within the basin.

****

'When I unleash the magic, they will know we are here,' Quila warned. 'Be ready.'

'We're ready,' Terin said. She would go first in to the pool, through the pipes into the Pyramid. Fast and sleek as an eel, her forceblades unaffected by the water, she would secure the foothold inside the building for the others.

The distant roar of explosions from the switching station.

'Diamond-clay bolts in the open,' Haram stated calmly. 'The enemy have taken the bait.'

'On my way.' Quila scurried out from the cover of the hedgerow.

Raptors swooped down towards her.

'They know we're here,' Haram snarled. His crossbows were wrapped in waterproof cloth, along with Birsin's crossbows. Quila couldn't fight off the Raptors and transform the Manta-spawn at the same time.

'The map,' Birsin said. 'They must have learned its secret.'

Lorak said nothing. He simply turned and began ripping apart the ornamental wall behind them, taking the skull-sized fragments of stone and throwing them at the Raptors with deadly accuracy.

Terin raced from cover, the glimmering steel of her forceblades flashing into life. She stood above her comrade Quila, prepared to die to protect her.

'Kirruk.' Birsin pointed at the far corner of the Pyramid, beyond the bridge.

'And behind us.' Birsin leapt forward to where the walls and hedgerows funnelled the enemy towards him.

'You deal with the lizards,' Lorak snapped at Haram. 'I'll deal with the birds.'

****

Soldat swam through the magic. His Scryer-marks nullified its corrosive effect, but it was hard to see, hard to breathe, every breath he took stolen from the air bubbling into the flow as it left the spell-gold pipe.

A shadow clawed at him, a naked soul torn away from the body of a lesser Mage. Soldat's Scryer-marks flared. He ripped the soul from his back and tore it into shreds of darkness which scattered behind him into the flow. He swam on. Too many dead added to the purified stream, not parsed into the flow by Zarak's sorcery. A corruption in the stream, a hindrance, but Soldat had a job to do and he intended to get it done.

Gasping, he forced himself forward, the magic heavy, cloying, the souls of the newly dead swirling around him. After he had destroyed his first attacker, the dead were more cautious and pushed tendrils of shadow into Soldat, too fine, too numerous for him to break them all.

They opened up their lives, their memories, their pain to him with vicious glee. They used their very deaths as a weapon.

So much pain, so much debasement. Some humans will do anything to survive, anything to make the random fortune of a totalitarian state pass on by, to pass on to another and leave them untouched. Soldat had only one defence against such misery. Felice couldn't reach him here, not until the full power of the connection formed, not until the strength of the others added to her own to drive through the foaming magic and link Soldat's mind to theirs. Only his own memories could stand bulwark against the raging pain of the newly dead.

Jani and his children: little Cara, tall Maran, funny Tesa. His children, his wife, his love for them, their love for him. He swam towards the pipe using their lives, their laughter as armour against the agony of the dead.

The pipe above him, he pulled himself upright and set his feet on solid footing. No air remained here in the middle of the flow. The dead were washed away by the force of the pouring magic; they couldn't bother him now.

But he had opened the floodgates of his mind to the memories of his wife, his children. Memories he had dammed up inside himself for so long. And he couldn't close them away again. Not here. Not like this.

He began chipping away at the walls around the pipe with a chisel.

Holding his breath.

Holding back his tears.

Holding the memory of his family close.

His will against the corruption of the magic.

****

'They know where the others stand,' Felice said, her voice calm in the maelstrom of battle. 'They can read the map.'

'Delightful.' Anria strove to keep her voice as steady as Felice's. 'Still enough Inoxit to go around, though.' She loosed two bolts in quick succession. The bolts struck two Inoxit in the centre of a talon. Exploding on contact, the clay sent shards of diamond through the insects. Shrapnel ripped into the other members of the talon. 'Haram has improved the mix.' Anria viewed the destruction. 'The clay wasn't as effective the last time, not against these creepy-crawlies anyway. Why are they so big? They move differently, too.'

'Rin plays with the design.' Felice loosed a single arrow that speared through one Inoxit into another, finally embedding itself in a third. The arrow was so finely aimed that it shredded the brains of each of the Inoxit in turn; the last fell twitching behind the corpses of its relatives. 'She's always playing at being a maker.'

'They are slower,' noted Anria.

'Yes.' Felice paused for a moment. It was time. 'Welcome to the family.' She opened the connection between them all.

We are one.

*****

'Without the map, we don't know where they will go.' Zarak slammed his hand flat upon the basalt. A dull booming sound rumbled through the chamber. 'Lorak is with them.'

'Ah, you fear his vengeance.' Rin chuckled. 'Families are so judgemental.'

'He should have died in the slave pits.'

'You should have killed him when you killed your parents. I would have.'

'I needed the money.'

'No matter,' Rin said. 'We know where they are now. I've sent my Callorts to kill them.'

'How do they hope to get through the Manta pool?' Zarak, with the information of the Raptors flooding into his mind, knew that the Shonri could only have one goal in mind. 'It makes no sense.'

Rin snarled. 'We will smash them there.'

****

Medina, safe within the protection of Gilbert's shadow, let the lumbering group of Callorts charge past her. Callorts could move with surprising speed, giving the lie to their bulk, but they always looked as if they lumbered.

She wondered where they were going. They were not heading towards the main gate or to any of the other entrances to the Pyramid, they were heading towards the spot where she saw the Shonri congregating on the map, but there was no entrance down in the bowels of the Pyramid.

Curiosity forced her to follow.

****

Quila, her hands in the water, grasped the back of a single Manta-spawn and held that struggling creature still as she sought the trigger, the switch, that place deep within it that changed it into a ravening, pearlescent white feeder on the flesh of its kin... There now, closer, there, deep within its tiny soul, the edge of the transformation.

She reached in with needles of magic. Her Scryer-marks blossomed gold against the silver while her comrades fought to keep her safe. Quila touched that essential mutation, flipping the switch, feeling the creature begin to change; but the switch had more than one setting, more than one outcome.

Quila had always assumed that it was the energy used to bring the Manta from a fish that swam through the sea to a ship that swam through the streams of magic in the air which blackened its skin, but this wasn't the case. The mutation was there, in the flesh of the Manta-spawn, from birth. She fought to keep the switch from flicking all the way over to Manta-ship, to the final outcome of the creature's distorted growth. There, she had it now. Under her control, the change surged out from this single spawn into all the others.

'We are one.'

Quila, Soldat, Haram, Lorak, Terin, Birsin, Anria, connected, interconnected, one mind, one consciousness, in the conduit formed by Felice's soul.

Lorak, throwing rocks at diving Raptors, hitting wings and bodies but occasionally managing to score a killing hit on the fast-moving skull, knowing without thought, without looking, which Raptors he could let fall to Terin's blades.

Terin, standing above the kneeling Quila, her forceblades weaving a skein of blood through the air, cutting through Raptors at the edge of their swoops, and slicing arrows from the air (there were human archers amongst the Kirruk forces); knowing when to leave a Raptor to Lorak's rocks, when to let an arrow pass unhindered, because she saw now with many eyes, her senses opened, tracking all that swirled around her.

Haram, his axe sweeping in graceful arcs, standing on the bridge, cutting down any Kirruk that dared to push towards him.

Birsin, at the edge of the gardens, spinning, leaping, blades appearing from the toes of his boots, from the heels, from his elbows, fists, knees, blades that clicked out, delivered a devastating blow and then disappeared again.

Anria, Felice, standing within the switching house, loosing arrows through the holes blasted through the walls, the Inoxit gaining ground even against that terrifyingly accurate arrow-storm, moving ever closer to overwhelming the station.

But Quila knew, they all knew, that Felice and Anria only sought to buy time for Soldat.

Soldat, the connection weak, but Quila could feel the pain of his memories, even as she pumped the transforming magic into the Manta pool with all her strength.

Soldat held himself upright against the flow of the magic cascading from the pipe and set the charges. Haram guided each step of the complicated procedure from nearly two miles away, even as Haram fought enemies only feet away from his face.

All one, all connected, all knowing what the others knew, without words, without thought, without sight or sound. Knowing in the same way they knew the movements of their own bodies.

The change coursed through the Manta-spawn, driven by the soul-power of eight Shonri connected to this single spot, the spot where Quila's hand met the water. The power washed out and into the Manta-spawn. Whose colours, whose responses to stimuli, changed, flickered wildly. From mottled drying blood where everything was food, to brilliant white where only their own flesh-kin were food, to jet black where magic itself was sustenance.

Blood, white, black.

Black, blood.

White.

Shining pearlescent white.

The Manta-spawn changed in an instant, attacking each other, lashing at each other with spiked, stinging tails, ripping at each other with jagged razor teeth.

A frenzy of feeding on the only food they desired.

Each other.

Terin cut a swooping Raptor out of the air, sheathed her blades and dived into the roiling surface of the Manta pool.

Soldat set a circle of charges around the spell-gold pipe. Under Haram's direction, he had set a single charge in the very centre of the flow. The wires embedded in the notches he had cut in the walls held the charge in place.

The folded-steel cone pointed back into the switching station, but a gleaming bulge of solidified Shonri electrum, that looked like nothing so much as a perfect blister, pointed up the pipe. So large it almost closed off the flow of the magic, but the wires held firm and the magic spurted around the shape of the charge.

Soldat, now that Haram was satisfied with the placement of the pinch charges, pushed away from the pipe. The shadows of the dead shied away from the connection of the Shonri, a connection that could tear their futile souls apart. He swam backwards through the strangely calm surface of the magic and dropped a single large satchel charge into the middle of the basin, equidistant to the walls of the switching station, which would cover over the damaged pipes with rubble and debris.

He sloshed to the edge of the basin and pulled himself out of the magic onto the stone floor behind Felice and Anria. He stood for a moment, letting the connection fully flower in his mind, letting the taint of the corrupted magic drain away from his soul. For that moment, all the Shonri heard the laughter of Jani, of his children… and the pain of their loss, before Soldat shut down that part of his mind, dammed up those memories once more, and the connection flooded with the solid intensity of his fury.

There was purity in Soldat's anger and they all basked in it.

Quila dove into the pool after Terin. Lorak ran to the edge of the water, the heavy weight of the electrum bomb balanced on one huge shoulder. The bomb wrapped in a waterproof sack filled with floatation bladders and attached to his belt by a Turmerix-woven cable.

Soldat retrieved his weapon harness from the floor. Slung it around his body, buckled it tight, and then knelt by the basin to set the last piece of the apparatus: the vibration detonator. It started to tick downwards. Nothing could stop a vibration detonator once set. The sympathetic magic connecting it to the explosives was impossible to neutralise.

'Thirty seconds.' The countdown ticked into the Shonri's minds.

Soldat picked up his repeating crossbow.

Birsin dived into the disturbed water of the Manta pool just in front of Lorak. Haram dived in just behind the mighty splash of Lorak's plunge. They let the force of the current pull them towards the pipes.

Soldat, Anria and Felice ran out of the switching station and into the massed Inoxit beyond.

'Twenty seven.'

The frenzied Manta-spawn, mostly white, but their colours flickered wildly and their responses changed from moment to moment. Those that were white had the edge in this battle, their purpose unambiguous. They attacked their kin to devour them, to grow.

A Manta-spawn striped black and white lunged at Haram. Haram ripped open its belly with the edge of his axe and three other pure-white spawn plunged into the swirling redness to tear the creature apart.

'Twenty five.'

CHAPTER NINETEEN

S ORA STRODE THROUGH THE WIDE CORRIDORS of the Pyramid, heading for the main gates. Her human bodyguards clustered around her, their weapons of magic-derived energy at the ready. Their eyes swept every shadow because Sora worried that Medina might be hiding there within her tame Gilbon's aura.

Sora studied the map as she walked. The Shonri were inside the Pyramid now, or at least under the walls, but their movements were strange, straggling out in a line as if they squeezed along a narrow corridor.

Had they found a secret entrance into the Pyramid, a tunnel that Zarak didn't know about? Did that tunnel exit near her? In her way? Blocking her escape?

She halted her bodyguards with a single thought. If the tunnel existed, the map would show it.

Standing still in the centre of a wide corridor, still three hundred yards from the main gate, she stared down into the map, pushing her gaze through its surface, to see the scene within the parchment.

****

'Twenty seconds.'

Terin, dolphin-like, leapt from the inner pool and somersaulted through the air. Her forceblades flashed clear of their scabbards and ignited as she landed on the flagstones inside the Pyramid, crouched, waiting for the attack that must surely come.

'Nineteen.'

Quila, fatigued by the spell-casting, tumbled in the current, struggled to the surface. The current dragged her towards the forcewall.

'Eighteen.'

Terin drove her forceblades into the flagstones, leaving them standing upright, as if buried in wood, spitting energy into the air. She yanked a coil of rope from her belt.

Birsin turned back against the current. Lorak caught fast in the pipe behind him. Their hands met in a gymnast's grip, hands grasping forearms, a solid unyielding strength.

'Seventeen.'

Terin threw the end of her rope straight into Quila's hands.

Anria snapped the sharp edge of her shield upwards through the mandibles of an advancing Inoxit and then on above her head to take the shock of a stooping Raptor. The force of the massive bird's attack drove her to her knees, but her sword stabbed into the Raptor's heart and then swept down to skewer the Inoxit with the sheered-off jaw.

'Sixteen.'

Terin realised that the arc of tension would still smash Quila into the forcewall. Not even a Shonri could survive that. There was no time to pull in the rope with her hands, so Terin ran in the opposite direction to the flow, away from her spitting forceblades, shortening the arc and saving Quila's life.

In the pipe behind the trapped Lorak, Haram cut through the silken cable attaching the bomb to the big Shonri's belt. He wrapped the cable around his fist and braced his feet against the pipe. Looking back as he prepared to push against Lorak's feet, he could see a mottled red, white, black and brown Manta-spawn trying to swim up the pipe towards him, but its growth spurt already made the creature too large to fit into the confined space.

Another Manta-spawn, blurred by the blood-pink water, tore into the creature. The two huge fish tumbled away into the frenzy of the outer pool.

'Fifteen.'

Soldat snapped the mechanism of his crossbow back and forth in a blur and emptied magazine after magazine of flaming death into the advancing Inoxit.

Birsin didn't have much air in his lungs, bubbles escaping his mouth as he heaved on Lorak's arm. Lorak had plenty of air left, but he blew it all out in a single breath to contract his ribcage and pull his shoulders inwards. Haram exhaled in one almighty heave.

Lorak popped free.

'Thirteen.'

Felice slung her bow across her back. Throwing-stars whistled from her hands, pealing like bells into the Raptors above. Blood splattered across her Scryer-cast skin.

The shortened arc of the rope smashed Quila into the edge of the pool. She clung there for a moment, gasping.

'Ten.'

Birsin surfaced for a moment, took one huge gulp of air and dived back under the surface. He swam past the rising Lorak, into the pipe, struggled against the current, caught hold of the slippery walls. Haram slammed into him.

'Nine.'

Birsin covered Haram's mouth with his own and blew life-giving air into his comrade's lungs.

Soldat, Anria and Felice reached the wall, a tall wall, solidly built, strong enough to protect them from the blast. They stood in its shadow and redoubled their efforts to clear a space around them. They didn't need much space; they just needed enough to allow them to leap over the wall. Anria stuck her sword into the face of an Inoxit, let go of the hilt, pulled a clay jar from her belt, threw it into the air, and retrieved her sword in time to cut through another Inoxit's arm.

'Seven.'

Haram and Birsin swam toward the surface, the heavy case of the electrum bomb bobbing along on the bottom behind them. The float-bladders not quite enough to give it positive buoyancy, but at least they neutralised most of the weight.

The clay jar reached the top of its arc and began to fall towards the ground.

'Six.'

Lorak reached down, pulled Haram to the surface by his hair and took the cable from his hand.

The clay jar struck the ground and exploded. A ripple of death through the Inoxit giving the three Shonri the space they needed.

Soldat flung his crossbow into the face of an Inoxit. Anria cut the head from the stunned creature. Felice leapt up and over the wall. The other two followed, grabbing the spikes atop the wall, swinging over, dropping down behind.

'*Four.*'

'Next time, measure,' Haram gasped at Birsin.

'Have you put on weight?' Birsin spluttered at Lorak.

'I had a big breakfast.'

Rin's Callorts chose that moment to attack and charged out of the corridor leading up into the Pyramid. Terin was twenty feet from her swords.

'*One.*'

Soldat, Anria and Felice covered their ears, opened their mouths, ignored the Inoxit clambering over the wall above them.

'*Zero.*'

Inside the switching station, the charge in the exact centre of the pipe exploded first. The cone held against the blast, driving the force of the explosion into the blister of electrum. Which vaporised and surged up the pipe towards the Pyramid, driving the magic before it. The pipe bulged but held, despite Haram's improvised calculations.

A microsecond later, the bracelet of charges around the pipe nipped it closed with implosive force.

Silence for a moment.

Then the huge charge in the centre of the holding basin erupted, smashing the switching station into shards of stone and metal. Shards whizzed through the air, ripping into the flesh of the Raptors and crushing the carapaces of the Inoxit. The wall collapsed upon Soldat, Anria and Felice. They ducked down, letting their armour take the damage, Anria's shield held above their heads.

In the basin, the magic was forced through the capillary pipes by the explosion. Magic mixed with the raging souls of the newly dead, the souls of those that magic had killed.

An unexpected occurrence.

The magic swept through the pipes and out into the city. A series of rapid retorts as glow-poles splintered, releasing the spirits of the newly dead into the air. The sun drove them back into the ground, into the bone pits, into the creeping darkness. Sparks from the splintered glow-poles ignited rubbish in the streets, burned people caught unawares, set fire to the wooden frames of the houses.

Witch-globes lifted into the air on the surge of raging energy tainted by awful death. The overpressure pumped the light of the witch-globes beyond the brilliance of white and up into the ultraviolet. Lashing heat poured down upon the city as the globes finally erupted into flame.

A column of black smoke rose from the burning city across the face of the sun.

****

Zarak barely had time to lift his hands from the surface of the basalt as the blast wave of magic slammed into the matrix of the stone, which pulsed with sparkling light but remained intact. The basalt held against the back-blast of magic by diverting it into the glowering walls. This surge of energy tipped the walls into a voracious hunger for more energy, more life force, more power.

The blast lifted Zarak, threw him across the chamber. He smashed into one of the walls and stuck there, three feet above the floor, the wall sucking at his armour's energy.

Rin wore no armour but the pain of her Inoxit as the explosion ripped them apart gave her a moment's warning. She ignored the agony lashing at her mind, grabbed the wooden table, pulled it over, and crouched behind it. The blast smashed the table to smithereens, but she survived—again.

The whole Pyramid vibrated under the force of the magic raging through the flame-white basalt. Internal walls crumbled. The weir to the Manta pool cracked, rocks tumbled down amongst the remaining Manta-spawn.

'Help me,' Zarak pleaded. He couldn't move. His armour already almost drained of energy. When it was exhausted, the walls would suck the life force from him.

Rin staggered to her feet. Splinters speckled her old skin with dots of blood. Blood that dripped onto her shawl, onto the floor. 'Help yourself.' She staggered out of the chamber on unsteady legs. The floor bucked beneath her feet.

Zarak groaned.

Chapter Twenty

THE MAGIC POURED THROUGH THE PYRAMID, through the internal channels that kept the lights blazing and powered the more esoteric equipment. The forcewall at the end of the inner pool cascaded sparks into the water before it failed and released the energy into the water.

Quila scrambled out of the energised water, still weak, still trying to focus. The floor snapped upwards towards her face.

That bounce in the floor saved Terin's life. She flexed as it hit, used it to throw herself into the air above the grasping hands of a Callort. She somersaulted sideways, kicked off another Callort's befuddled head, and landed by her swords. She ripped them free of the floor and rolled away from a clumsy kick.

The weight of the Callorts meant that they could ride out the waves of energy buckling the floor underneath them, but that very mass made their movements on the unstable surface slower than normal. Stability came at a price.

Terin lunged upright; her blades sounded a symphony of death, shearing through Callort skin as if it were parchment. Black blood sprayed through the air, a fine mist through which Terin danced as the floor continued to vibrate beneath her.

Birsin and Haram clambered out of the pool before the magic ripped into them. They drew sharp knives and set to work cutting at the waterproof cloth covering their crossbows.

Quila lay stunned, the screaming agony of the magic slashing through her brain, overriding the connection, overriding everything, but she still managed to fumble a clay jar from her belt and hurled it at the Callorts crowding through the doorway.

Lorak took the full force of the magic flooding through the pool.

He spasmed rigid from the pain, but didn't let go of the cable to the electrum bomb.

The energy wave flushed through the pipes into the Manta pool beyond, throwing the struggling mass of Manta-spawn into the open river while driving raging magic into their quivering flesh.

Terin skipped sideways, her blades flickering through the dark mist of Callort blood. She couldn't keep this up for long. Not long enough for Birsin and Haram to free their crossbows.

Quila's clay jar exploded, throwing shards of diamond in a spray of shrapnel. Terin used the two Callort before her as a shield against the blast; they stumbled, staggered, their internal organs scythed through by the shards.

The door blocked but only for a moment and there were still too many Callorts left standing for Terin to stay alive, unless she gave up the defence of her comrades, her family, unless she chose to move, to dance away, to leave the others to fend for themselves.

And that would never happen.

In the river, the Manta-spawn ate anything that came within range of their hungry mouths. The river fish consumed in moments and now the spawn, some nearly twenty-feet long, returned to hunting each other. This battle would end when only one Manta remained. An outcome programmed into their brains, their minds, their bodies.

In the inner pool, which the Manta would never see again, Lorak surged from the water. The cable held fast in his hand. He yanked the electrum bomb up, swung the heavy case around his head, and yelled a wild battle cry.

Terin leapt, her back arched over the whirling cable. Quila rolled into a depression created by the stone-splitting force of the magical blast. The cable brushed her face. Haram and Birsin dived back into the water. Haram couldn't quite believe what Lorak intended to do even though the power of the connection left him in no doubt.

A second time the bomb whirled around Lorak's head. Terin leapt again as the others stayed down, letting the cable whoosh by above their heads.

The mass of the electrum bomb in its brassbound case, in its waterproof bag stuffed full of float bladders, smashed into the Callorts at knee height, to the ripping sound of float-bladders bursting.

Callorts tumbled like monoliths in an earthquake.

Terin continued the movement of her second leap. Her blades cut down into two fallen Callorts.

Lorak let go of the cable. The electrum bomb skidded away across the floor in its tattered waterproof sack and clattered into the wall. He pulled the cestus gloves from his belt, yanked them on. Flexed his fists. Spikes clicked out over his knuckles.

Lorak didn't dance.

He smashed his way into the Callorts, Terin pirouetting behind him, protecting his back. Haram pulled himself out of the water, tossed a crossbow to Birsin and finished preparing his own. He rotated the arms of the bow, snapped them down into their housing, yanked back the string, and fitted a magazine of diamond-clay bolts into place.

Quila's strength returned with Shonri swiftness. She drew a foot-long baton from her belt. Twisted it. Click, and the baton became a staff. Another click, and blades of folded steel extended from both ends of the staff.

The fight didn't take long after that.

****

When the surge of magic died away, the basalt slab faded to reflective black.

With a sigh, the walls released Zarak, dropped him in a crumpled heap upon the floor. He lay there unmoving for a moment, sapped of life, his magicked youthfulness drained away. Somehow, he staggered to his feet. His aged legs trembled under the weight of his exhausted armour. Liver spots clustered across his hands, his face. Blue veins visible under his wrinkled skin.

He tottered forward. His heart thudded reluctantly in his chest. Blood pulsed sluggishly through his arteries. A rushing filled his ears. Breath wheezed through his drooling mouth. His suddenly yellow teeth clattered on the stones, falling loose from his ancient, receding gums.

Another tottering step.

Pain stabbed at his left arm, lanced up into his shoulder, tightened across his chest. A fist of pain closed around his heart.

'Ahhhh…'

He collapsed, one fingertip touching the basalt; too late, far too late for the magical energy to repair the damage. He couldn't speak. He couldn't make a single sound. Crushing weight upon his chest. Breath sighed out of him for the last time.

The basalt drained his sordid soul and dumped it into the catacombs beneath the city. Where the souls of the dead, the source of his power, those he had enslaved and abused even into the afterlife, tore it to shreds.

The smoke rising from the burning houses grew thicker, blacker against the rays of the sun.

****

'Zarak's dead,' Felice said.

'How do you...? The Raptors.' Anria looked up. The huge birds flapped away from the city, released from their bondage. Some, their wings outstretched, caught the thermals rising from the burning city.

'Lorak won't be happy,' Soldat said.

Anria pulled the thought from the connection, still burbling away behind their minds, though dimmed, no longer needed for combat. 'Zarak is Lorak's brother,' Anria said. 'He cast Lorak into slavery.'

'Yes,' Felice said. 'And Lorak knows that he can never have his vengeance now.'

None of the Inoxit survived the explosion. Their shattered bodies were scattered around the switching station and the foul stench of their blood corrupted the air.

'There are still Kirruk down there,' Soldat said. 'They will fight on even if Zarak is dead. They don't know how to do anything else.'

'They'll be attacking the city folk now.' Anria gazed out at her city, at the place that birthed her. People streamed out onto the streets, rushing away from their homes, their lives, carrying nothing with them. Why? Why the rush? There were not enough Kirruk alive down there to cause such panic. People didn't discard their possessions so lightly.

It was only just gone noon, hours yet before night fell and the dead crept out into the sunless dark.

Anria looked up again, at the dark billowing smoke beginning to obscure the sun. She said, 'We don't have much time.'

Soldat picked his repeating crossbow out of the shattered remnants of an Inoxit skull and slung it over his back, all the magazines depleted in the defence. He unshipped the heavy crossbow, snapped the double steel arms into place, set his foot in the stirrup and drew back the string, but he didn't set a bolt into the groove, because he didn't know what kind of ammunition he would require.

'You lead, Anria,' Felice said. 'You know these streets.'

The three Shonri raced down into the burning city towards the Pyramid, they still had to complete their mission and destroy the map. The others still needed their help.

*****

Quila brushed the tears from Lorak's face. To learn of Zarak's death, like this, in a stray thought sent through the connection. All those years, decades, of vengeance spent in a moment.

'I wanted to crush his skull between my hands,' Lorak whispered.

'I know, my love.' Quila placed her arms around his neck and hugged his head close. 'I know.'

'He killed our parents, sold me into slavery, all so he could buy his way into a Mage's good graces.'

'I know.'

'I wanted to kill him, tear his head from his body, smash everything he built and spit in his dying eyes.'

'I know.'

Lorak breathed in her scent. It calmed him. His eyes flickered shut. 'At least the bastard's dead.' He stood, lifting her from the ground. His arms around her as they kissed. Lorak smiled his way out of the kiss. 'Sod him to hell.'

Haram examined the bomb. The casing had cracked, but the bomb itself seemed intact. He'd have to open the case to be sure, but first... 'Are you good?' he asked Lorak.

Lorak released Quila. 'I'm good.'

'So what part of bomb don't you understand?'

'It survived,' Lorak said. 'I knew it would. I took the percentage chances from your mind.'

'Percentage?' Terin checked over her forceblades. This she had to hear.

Haram held up one finger. 'The percentage chance that the float-bladders would not cushion the blow.' He held up another finger. 'That the cloth would not cushion the blow.' Three fingers. 'That the casing would not split open.' Four fingers. 'That the stasis sphere would not destabilise.' Haram closed his hand into a solid fist. 'That it would not all go…' he opened it again into a splay of fingers '…boom.'

'What were the percentages?' Birsin asked.

'All told, all totted up?' Lorak asked.

'Yes.'

'Seventy/thirty.'

Birsin said nothing for a moment, then, 'Next time, we spend a whole lot longer planning.'

Medina watched it all from the protection of Gilbert's shadow.

Chapter Twenty-One

S ORA ROLLED UP THE MAP. The Shonri had found a weakness in Zarak's defences. She wasn't surprised, but neither was she worried. They didn't stand between her and the main entrance, which was all that mattered. Let Rin and Zarak fight them off if they could. She would escape with the map and the key to seeing what it showed. She'd hold that knowledge, the knowledge of where the Shonri leaders travelled, and could use it to make herself leader of the Twelve.

No Lamia had ever risen so high.

Not even Cinome.

She smiled, triumphant, and looked towards her escape.

Calderan stood at the end of the corridor with flames behind his eyes. Flames Sora could see. The air shimmered around his face. Sora's bodyguards shifted nervously, raising their weapons, but she felt nothing but contempt for the Fire-mage's petty display.

'I'd thought you'd fled by now,' she said, derision dripping acid into her words. 'Zarak won't be impressed if he finds you still in his keep.'

Calderan didn't reply. Flames coiled along his arms to his glowing hands.

'Nothing to say, Caldie?' Sora deliberately used her pet name for him. This was so very tiresome. 'No begging for me to return to your bed?'

Calderan's head dropped.

Sora sneered; he really was quite pathetic. With a single thought, she commanded her bodyguards to move.

Flames curled through the air above Calderan's head. He raised his gaze to Sora's face. She realised her error. His eyes, his hellish eyes, no pupil, no cornea, just an inferno of hate.

'Calderan!' she screamed.

Her screams were lost in the roar of the furnace as Calderan thrust out his hands towards her. A roar modulated into a screech of jealousy, of self-loathing, flowing from Calderan's blazing mouth.

The conflagration swept along the corridor towards her. The very walls of the Pyramid melted in the heat, runnels of molten rock puddled on the floor. Sora's bodyguards shrieked as the fire consumed them, but only for a moment. Vapourised by Calderan's unleashed fury.

Sora smelled her flesh burning, felt her eyes melt in their sockets, gasped in the flame which scorched down her throat to her lungs—but her magic held long enough for her to release her hold on this dying body, to let her soul flee—and find a new host.

The corridor floor melted beneath her, dripping like candle wax into the corridors below. The map gone, nothing left of it now, not even ash. Such a shame, but she had seen the places where the Shonri congregated in their travels. She knew where the Twelve should look for the Machine. She still held a bargaining chip.

Sora slipped into the body of one of Zarak's slaves, the struggle for control brief. She smiled from behind new eyes. The pain of burning alive was intense, quite draining; she'd have to recover before she fled the Pyramid.

Calderan smashed into the room. 'I will burn every body you inhabit,' he screeched.

The flame lashed out and Sora screamed.

****

Haram opened the bomb and inspected its inner workings. Lorak stood guard above him with Quila guarding *his* back. Terin and Birs-in scouted along the passageways leading up into the Pyramid. They didn't have much time. The Magi who remained would seek to escape with the map and the decision about the bomb had to be made now. Should they use it?

The city burned outside the Pyramid, an unexpected result of the destruction of the switching channel. Haram realised that this was mostly his fault. He had been over-exuberant with the explosives, overly keen to see what they could do. Well, he knew now: they could burn a city to the ground.

Out in the streets, Soldat flicked his flexible saw around the neck of a Kirruk. Yanked it back. The teeth cut through the lizard flesh, through the bone, removing the head as Soldat lashed the saw around like a whip. Green blood spurted from the forlorn neck as the Kirruk head bounced away across the cobbles.

Soldat wanted to get to the Pyramid to stop any Magi from escaping with the map, but this city had suffered enough. *'No,'* he mind-sent. *'The bomb must wait for another day.'*

Anria cut open the bowels of a Kirruk with the wicked edge of her shield. A company of the lizardmen blocked their path to the Pyramid and Soldat elected not to go around them. Anria hadn't argued against the decision. She thrust her sword into a Kirruk throat. *'I agree. We have done enough to these people.'*

Within the Pyramid, Terin jogged forward, checking out a side-corridor as Birsin held the intersection. *'I agree.'*

Lorak, Haram, and Quila acquiesced.

Birsin squatted in the corridor guarding Terin's back. He knew the rule. The decision must be unanimous. He called back Terin. She sprinted along the corridor as he walked back into the chamber of the Manta pool. The corpses of twenty Callorts lay cooling on the broken floor. The walls cracked into a broken mosaic of crumbling concrete by the explosive force of diamond clay.

Terin entered the chamber and shared a glance with Lorak, Haram, and Quila. They all knew Birsin's cold edge. He had good reason to despise the people of this city, having lived amongst their petty viciousness for years.

Would he agree?

'Very well.' He didn't speak, he couldn't speak, the words would make him vomit with despair. These humans, these people they protected would see them dead in an instant for the price of a hot meal. He'd heard their poisonous thoughts spoken aloud, watched them bow and scrape to the Magi. Yet... he could not watch everything burn. *'Another time.'*

'It is agreed?' Felice asked.

'It is agreed,' they responded.

'Oh I don't think I agree.' Medina stepped out of Gilbert's shadow. 'I don't think I agree at all.'

****

'You?' Haram, who had been so forceful in his lust, gazed at her with shock in his eyes.

'Medina?' Lorak, surprisingly gentle in his lovemaking. Had he ever told his love Quila, her hands so soft, so skilled, about his dalliance? Had Quila ever told him?

'Where were you hiding?' Terin blushed; such a passionate lover.

'Nerina.' Birsin stumbled backwards, tripped over the outstretched leg of a Callort corpse, clung to the wall to save himself from falling. 'I thought you dead. I thought Basilard had forced your death. I killed him for it and laughed as he died.'

Soldat staggered in the middle of his fight with the few remaining Kirruk. Medina smiled. He'd been so very sweet. He'd actually worried about hurting her.

'No,' Felice whispered into the connection.

Anria leapt past Soldat and killed a Kirruk before it could bring its sword down upon Soldat's head. She dropped to a crouch, her shield extended, spinning about her heel, slashing through Kirruk legs, then rising and killing them as they lay howling on the floor. 'All of you?' she asked in disbelief. 'All of you?' The last Kirruk died with Anria's sword through its heart.

'Hello, Felice,' Medina whispered into the connection. 'Did you miss me?'

Lying on silk, two bodies entwined, touching, tasting, slicked skin glistening in the lamplight, wind sighing through open windows, the connection between the two magnificent in its completeness. Two Conduits combined into one soul upon sweat-soaked sheets.

All saw, all understood; even Anria felt the pain of it. Of the betrayal.

Birsin, his heart breaking anew, threw other images into the mix. He had loved Nerina, loved her with all his heart and thought her dead.

'Love unreturned is not love.' Medina cast his rampant imagery aside.

All saw, all felt Birsin's grief and their attempt, their instinctive human attempt to soothe his pain, to touch his soul with theirs, allowed Medina to drive her own images into their minds. Felice had sent a mind-blast along that same connection all those years ago, killed their sister Conduits, their family. Only Nerina survived. She took a new name, Medina, took the vials she had filled with the juice of Birsin and Felice—for even then she toyed with sympathetic magic—and hid herself away to recover her strength.

The Shonri collapsed, unable to control their bodies or even move their eyes, trapped in the web of Medina's craft.

'The juice of our love saved me that day, Felice. It glowed so hot when you prepared your treachery, allowed me to defend my soul against your betrayal. Now it will tear aside your lies… my love.'

Two Conduits on that silk, making love with their minds open to each other. Every caress, every kiss, every moment linking one to the other, flowing between them, rising… rising… to a climax that rivalled the stars in the sky.

Bursting from them in white heat, such love, such power, so connected, so free, so truthful, so much agony when Felice blasted death along that same conduit.

They had been Basilard's favourites. He took pleasure from them when he wished. They took pleasure from each other when they could.

One body, one orgasm, on and on, their souls conjoined in ecstasy.

Anria lay outside that personal linkage, that oh-so-personal linkage. No vial of *her* juices lay in Medina's control, but the edge of her mind shivered at what Medina revealed. What were these Old Ones? The Seven? What had they done?

'We were one,' Medina hissed into the connection.

Anria quailed at the quality of that aching thought, the ache of a lover discarded.

'One spirit, one soul, one mind, one Shonri, and you cast me aside, tried to burn my mind from existence.'

Even on the edge of this connection, Anria could feel the power of Medina's spell-craft. Birsin linked to her. Haram linked to Felice. Medina and Felice two poles of power, the others like moths, burned by a flame they hadn't even known existed.

'You were never Shonri,' Felice cried back into the connection. *'The Machine refused you the gift.'*

'I was a Conduit. I felt them fight, die, kill. Was that not Shonri enough?'

The smoke rose above the city, the winter sun dropped towards nightfall, the dead grew restive in the catacombs below the city, and Soldat and Felice crumpled on the ground, unmoving. Their eyes open but seeing nothing. Their hands empty of weapons. Their Scryer-marks faded away to almost nothing. The dead would take their souls and leave nothing but husks behind.

Anria cursed and turned at a sound behind her. Her sword raised. Her shield lifted to protect her face. Over its razor-sharp edge, she saw a man leading his wife and children to safety. His gaze met Anria's and his fear burned her aware. Not fear for himself, but fear for those he loved.

'Go,' she snarled. 'Run. We do this for you. Now run, before the Magi return to enslave you again.'

The man nodded his head and hustled his family away.

This still left Anria with the problem of what to do with her friends. What could she do? She wasn't an Old One. They might call her family, but she wasn't one of them, not really. She hadn't fought in the rebellion with them. Their shared memories weren't her shared memories. Their jokes weren't her jokes. Their history wasn't her history.

No way into the binding spell of Medina's vengeance. At that moment Anria was an outsider.

The man picked up his youngest daughter when she fell and carried her away into the gloom.

A whispered conversation on those silken sheets in the midst of exhausted passion. Felice had tried to convince Nerina... Medina that Soldat was right, that the Shonri and their sisters of the Conduit should rise up against Basilard.

Medina had giggled at the suggestion. Why would she want that? There was so much pleasure still to be had here on the sweat-slicked sheets and out there on the blood-soaked battlefields. She could live behind the eyes of the Shonri, live on the deaths they inflicted, revel in their sacrifices.

'You were not what I thought.' Birsin spoke into the connection.

'Of course not.' Medina's contempt caused all pain. *'I was a Conduit, you were merely Shonri.'*

'I thought I had destroyed you,' Felice cried out, her pain reborn.

'No, you freed me.' Medina chuckled.

Her mind torn open by Felice's treacherous attack, only the knowledge of the sympathetic magic, which she'd torn from the mind of a dying Witch years earlier, allowed her to survive. Cast into waves of pain, finding her way out through pathways unopened in the human mind until that day. The heated vials guided her path. She changed, became Medina. As time went on, the Old Ones of the Shonri came to her for healing and she harvested their life forces, storing them in vials, for no real reason at all.

'Soldat was the last of my conquests, so difficult to persuade. He thought that he might hurt me.'

Anria reeled at her sudden revelation. Soldat had lied, to Medina, to himself, his concern for the Witch a brick in the wall of a dam. The dam held back the broken grief of his bereavement. Anria closed her eyes against the sight of her city burning and the shame of what she was about to do. She had no love to share, no grief to use to break the spell cast over her new family, but Soldat the Indomitable, the righteous anger at the heart of the rebellion, the Shonri who wouldn't stop, had love enough to shatter the world.

She hoped he would forgive her.

Anria forced her mind into the connection, through Medina's gleeful spite. She found the memories of Jani, of Maran, of Tesa, of Cara. She lifted them from Soldat's paralysed mind, formed them into a wedge, the laughter, the pain, the terrible loss, the broken church, the silent village, the cloying softness of the loam, the smell of fresh-cut grass, the flowers, the terrible scent of death.

'Get out of my head!' Soldat roared as his Scryer-marks flared gold, such power in his anger; a power that forged the connection anew. Lorak and Quila, joined by their love, responded first, pushing their own wedges into the cracks appearing in Medina's spell. Terin's blistering speed of thought lashed at the Witch. Haram craftily broke her power on the back of his love for Felice.

'She's a clever one, that new Shonri,' Medina whispered into Felice's mind. *'Until we meet again, my love.'*

The link snapped.

Soldat rolled over onto his knees, scooped up his weapons, stood with his back to Anria.

'Thank you,' he said, without looking at her.

Felice wept.

****

Haram raised his head. The connection renewed but he didn't want to trust his mind to it, not with Medina still about. Medina! He leapt to his feet, the axe in his hands.

He couldn't see her.

Haram looked to the bomb. Somebody had closed the case. It could only be Medina. Haram's head drooped, he knew what she'd done.

'We didn't even get beyond our foothold,' Lorak said.

'We still need to find the map.' Quila kissed him softly on the cheek.

'Bitch,' Birsin muttered.

'Correct,' Medina whispered in Gilbert's untraceable voice. 'The map is destroyed. Burned, I think, by the feel of the spell. I'm glad. So much better for you to keep your secrets. Don't you think?'

Terin drew her forceblades. 'Keep talking.' She tilted her head to one side, listening, trying to pinpoint Medina's position.

'I think Haram has something to tell you.' Medina's laugh faded away.

'She's set the detonator,' Haram said.

Chapter Twenty-Two

SORA FLED INTO ANOTHER BODY, so exhausted by the constant battles to steal a host that she barely had enough strength left to drive this soul out, but she managed and staggered away through the gloom. Pillars of smoke rose from the houses. No sunlight reached this part of the city now. Dark shadows swirled out of the ground around the Lamia, but they avoided her power and went after easier flesh.

Too many people had waited for the Magi to solve the problem, waited as the smoke rose to obscure the sun, waited as darkness fell and the dead rose.

Calderan hunted her through the city streets. How could he find her? How did he know which body she inhabited? Had his madness given him powers unknown?

Flame lashed at her new body. 'I'll burn you forever,' Calderan cried.

The dead shied away from the brightness of Calderan's vengeance. Sora, desperate, leapt into the body of a horse, a creature never meant to hold the soul of a Magi. The pain tore at the edges of her sanity. She couldn't stay here.

Casting herself adrift once more, expecting this to be the last time—that she'd dissipate into nothingness—she spotted a young man. Lamias preferred to remain female—no man could ever become a Lamia—but they could take a male body. Femininity was a preference, not a law of nature.

This young man appeared fit, strong; maybe this body could run fast enough to get away from Calderan. The horse failed because it couldn't contain her soul, but this man's body could, if she could only steal it in her weakened state.

She focussed her will, the incredible will of a Lamia, the will of a soul that wouldn't allow death to be its end. She made her will a weapon, a lance, a blade of terrible swiftness. She lashed with whip-crack ferocity into the man.

She expected a battle—men's souls were so attached to their bodies, their physicality defining them—but instead the soul gave up the body. The young man thanked her and floated away towards oblivion.

With dread like ice on the spine, Sora realised her mistake.

The dead already swirled around the legs of this body, trapping it here, their tendrils sunk into its soul. The very soul she broke free of its moorings and replaced with her own. Such focus in her will, such swiftness in her strike, exhausted her. She couldn't break free.

More came, pouring over the ground. They had trapped another Mage. Zarak! They had torn Zarak to shreds. Sora fought, struggled, used all her guile, but she failed; flattened by so many transitions, depleted by so many battles, she couldn't escape the dead.

Calderan laughed and withheld his fire, his cleansing fire, the fire that would release her from this torment. 'It seems the dead can kill a Lamia.'

Sora wailed. Her soul, the soul that had stolen so many lives, dragged down into the cloying dark beneath the city.

****

'Can't you stop it?' Terin said, staring at the bomb.

Haram shook his head. 'Vibration detonator. Once set, it can't be stopped. It can't even be removed. It and the bomb are linked in a sympathetic relationship. The Turmerix called it an entangled relationship. Doesn't matter how far away from the bomb the detonator is, once it reaches zero, the bomb explodes.'

He couldn't drop the information into their minds, because none of them was willing to trust their mind to the connection. Medina was still out there with those damn vials. They hadn't discussed how she'd filled all those vials, either. Quila looked askance at Lorak. He shrugged and raised an eyebrow. She blushed and looked away. Then they held hands.

They were holding hands still. 'How long?' Lorak asked the pertinent question.

'Fifty minutes, no…' Haram squinted at the dial. 'Forty-six minutes.'

'Plenty of time to get away,' Birsin said. 'You said a quarter mile, right?'

'If the bomb goes off here… so close to the outer wall of the Pyramid…'

'We need to move the bomb then,' Quila said.

'It's a vibration detonator. One slip, one stumble might set the bomb off.'

'And you designed this into the bomb,' Terin said. 'Why?'

'Because I didn't want the Magi to be able to stop it,' Haram snapped.

'Okay,' Quila said. 'Calm down all of you. This isn't the only mistake we've made today.'

'That's comforting,' Terin said.

'I can carry it.' Lorak rolled his shoulders. 'I can carry it to the centre of the Pyramid. That's where you said it should go.'

A brief silence.

'Not a slip. Not a stumble.' Birsin spat on the floor. 'We're not monks. Why should we care if the city is destroyed?'

'You don't have to stay,' Lorak rumbled.

'If you stay, I stay.'

'We all stay.' Terin took a deep breath. 'And we have to try.'

****

Anria took careful aim at the clump of Kirruk guarding the main entrance to the Pyramid. It was her last diamond-clay bolt. After this, she was out of ammo for her crossbows.

She squeezed the trigger.

The bolt exploded in the middle of the enemy. Anria and Soldat charged into the smoke. It took bare seconds to kill the last of them.

'Why haven't they deserted?' Anria asked.

'There's still light here,' Soldat said. 'The dead lie in wait out there in the dark. What has happened here?' Large holes blasted in the sides of the Pyramid, steep slopes of stone scarred by streams of molten rock.

The lights still shone in the Pyramid because the power disrupted at the switching station still worked here at its source, but no lights flickered in the City of Lights. The City of the Dead, Anria thought, the City of Ghosts.

The city burned ferociously in places, the firelight kept the dead away, but there was more than enough darkness for their hunting. This left the living a choice: flee along the lines of fire and risk being crisped by the flames, or flee into the cool darkness and risk being consumed by the dead.

'We need to find the others and get out of this city,' Soldat said.

'I can't feel them,' Felice whispered. 'They've closed their minds to me.'

'We have to move, Felice,' Soldat said gently. 'We have to move now.'

'I can't feel them.'

'I'll scout ahead,' Anria said. She could feel the lack of the connection like an aching hole in her soul. How must it feel to Soldat? To Felice? Medina had broken something here that might never be rebuilt.

'I'll bring her.' Soldat wiped a hand across his eyes. He looked weary. 'Don't go too far into the Pyramid.'

Anria nodded. 'I'll leave sign,' she said and jogged up the steps into the Pyramid. Nothing moved in the main corridor, so she scratched an arrow into the wall with a dagger to mark her direction of travel and moved forward.

Where were the others?

****

Birsin killed a Callort with his last explosive bolt and loaded his last magazine of folded steel into the crossbow. He knelt in the corridor and waited for Terin to move past him.

****

Terin jogged past Birsin. He pointed at his crossbow as she passed and signed negation. No more diamond clay then. They might be reduced to hand signals and voice, but they were still Shonri, still the best fighters left in this broken world.

But she felt the emptiness where Felice's touch always resided.

A squad of Kirruk stood guard at the next intersection, a lesser Mage commanding them, still holding his post despite the confusion and the panic, either loyal, stupid, or both. At the very least, his behaviour showed a distinct lack of imagination.

Terin drew her forceblades and sprinted along the corridor. The Mage looked up. Terin cut him open from shoulder to hip. She danced through the Kirruk for a moment.

Then whistled the all clear to Birsin.

****

Quila passed Birsin's hand signal back to Haram and Lorak.

Sweat poured down Lorak's face. The weight of the bomb balanced in his hands. He took one step, and then another, using his mighty musculature to smooth out any vibration.

Quila swept the floor of rubble and cleared any corpses out of the way as she moved forward. She pointed out any unevenness in the floor to Lorak, tried to ease his path. If he stumbled, if he fell, then all ended in a single moment. Which was why she wouldn't leave his side, wouldn't scout ahead; she'd be here with him whatever happened.

Behind Lorak, Haram was supposed to be acting as rearguard, but his gaze never left the bomb.

Quila smiled encouragement at Lorak.

From along the corridor, Birsin signalled the all-clear.

****

'What in hell's name happened here?' Soldat said when he and Felice caught up with Anria. A slagged corridor blocked their path. Waves of heat shimmered from the melted stone. 'We can't go that way.'

'This corridor leads down,' Anria said. 'But we don't know which way to go.'

'I don't know where they are,' Felice cried out. 'I can't feel them. Don't you understand? I can't feel them.'

Anria glanced across the molten floor. Something there? That shadow. It looked wrong. Where was the light source?

Medina stepped from the shadow, a vicious little smile on her lips. 'Oh poor little Felice, lost your darling family, have you?' She pouted. 'So sad.'

Anria didn't hesitate, swinging her shield in a fast arc, sending it spinning along the corridor. Its razor edge glimmered in the red heat of the molten stone.

Medina just managed to duck in time. The shield sliced a hank of hair from her head, blood splattering from the gash in her scalp.

Gilbert gasped as the shield scythed through his torso, cutting him in two, but as he died, as his blood rushed from his body in a gout of stinking mess, he released his shadow, his mind-clouding power, to protect the woman who had eaten his soul.

The wall of darkness lasted only moments, but it was enough. Medina's mocking laughter faded as she fled.

'So that's what the bitch looks like through my eyes,' Anria said. 'Good to know.' She spotted the hank of Medina's hair on the other side of molten stone. Glancing at Felice, she remembered something she'd read once as a child, something about sympathetic magic.

She jogged back up the corridor, away from the molten floor. Turned. Took a deep breath and sprinted towards the shimmering heat.

Anria knew she couldn't make the leap, but she could do something else. Her Scryer-marks flared within her skin. Faster she sprinted, faster, leaping off the floor, running along the wall, the heat of the molten stone singeing her hair. Hitting the floor beyond, rolling to a halt.

She stepped over the blood of the Gilbon and picked up the bloody hank of Medina's hair. Tucking it inside her armour, she examined her shield, buried in the wall to half its diameter. She tried to pull it free, but it was stuck fast and she only managed to cut her hand on its edge.

Looking down at her hand, she noted absently that her Scryer-marks had thickened, strengthened, become more pronounced within her skin.

Then she repeated her crossing of the molten floor and strode across to the weeping Felice. She pulled out Medina's hair. 'Find them. Her blood is here. Use it to find our family.'

Chapter Twenty-Three

F ELICE HELD THE PIECE OF BLOODY HAIR, the ache in her soul tearing at her concentration.

'Find them,' Anria said. 'They need you.'

Felice hesitated, glanced at Soldat.

'Find them, Felice,' he said. 'Please.'

Tears dried on Felice's cheeks, she looked at the hair, so much pain. The memory of killing her sisters, of sending that blast of magic surging through the connection all the Conduits shared, a connection that could not be closed down, that could not be denied, but Nerina... no, Medina... she called herself Medina now... had escaped that blast. Medina, freed by mental energy, became a true Witch.

They were supposed to be a myth, Witches, something lost to the world. What else remained that should be lost? Sympathetic magic: the magic of resonances, of essences, the magic of the aether. Felice cleared her mind of grief, of pain, and pulled forth the memory of her sisters' minds burning out—a sensation that had destroyed Felice's sanity for long years. She held that memory tight, pulled it into focus, felt it again. The screams, the pain, the cold onrushing darkness. She let the memory go, let it float away from her consciousness, focussed in on the one soul that survived.

Medina's sweat drenched that chunk of hair, perfumed it. Move past the pain, through the misery, through the madness into the aether beyond, into the place where Medina hid. Find the link, the link between Medina and the connection; through her Felice could find her family again.

Look.

Deeper.

Deeper.

There.

Felice's joy bloomed in the touch of her family. She smiled at Soldat, at Anria.

'Where are they?' Soldat asked.

'They're heading for the central chamber. They carry the bomb.' Felice's joy faded into terror. 'It's armed.'

'What's the quickest way? Felice. Don't lose yourself again.' Anria gripped her arm. 'Find the route. Medina knows it. Find the route.'

Felice smiled again. She could read Medina's memories, her knowledge of the Pyramid, from the sympathetic magic of the Witch's hair.

****

Lorak's arms trembled. The weight of the bomb not a problem, but holding it steady, holding it so not a single vibration transferred itself to the detonator, took every ounce of his strength. His back ached, the muscles of his abdomen twitched, his forearms tightened in cramp, and still he took another step.

He couldn't afford to place the bomb upon the ground even for an instant. To carry it simply meant to keep his body locked, leaving his joints to balance out the vibrations of his steps—but to lower it, to bend his aching knees, to control its descent to the floor, that might well be impossible.

Haram and Birsin would have to lower the bomb. All Lorak needed to do was carry it to the chamber.

He took another step.

And another.

Birsin jogged back from scouting ahead. 'Not far now. Twenty yards, no more.'

Lorak didn't look up. He couldn't spare the energy. 'How long?'

'Twenty minutes or thereabouts,' Haram said.

'Long enough,' Lorak said and took another step.

****

Medina could sense Felice scratching at the surface of her mind. So the Conduit had discovered the aether. Should she show the woman what it could do? No, let her discover it for herself.

She picked up a Raptor feather from the ground in front of her. The sun faded into twilight, but the dark forms of the dead avoided her. They sensed that she was a Witch, that she ate souls.

'Time to leave,' Medina said. She let Felice take the map of the Pyramid from her mind and then closed down the connection for good. Blood caked across one side of her face, but the gouge in her scalp had already healed over. When her hair grew back, the power of the strands that Felice held would vanish, because Felice didn't know how to preserve such things.

That new one, that Anria, had proved fast, strong, clever.

A smile of joy.

'I do so love a challenge.' Medina lifted the Raptor feather to her lips and kissed it.

****

Haram halted just inside the door to the central chamber. Lorak's gaze focussed on something beside the basalt slab. Haram glanced across: a desiccated corpse, one hand outstretched, touching the slab. The armour revealed the corpse's identity.

Zarak.

Lorak's brother.

'Birsin!' Haram shouted. 'Grab it.' He leapt forward, reaching out, getting his hands under the case. Birsin barely reached the other side in time. Lorak, exhausted, faced with the sight of his hated brother's corpse, released the weight before Birsin managed to achieve a proper grip.

Then Soldat was there, skidding under the bomb case, letting it rest on his shoulders, grunting as he took the weight of the bomb.

Birsin adjusted his grip.

'Have you got it?' Soldat spoke through gritted teeth.

'Yes,' Birsin said.

Haram nodded. He couldn't speak past the sheer terror of what had almost happened.

'Hurry,' Birsin gasped.

The two Shonri lifted the bomb smoothly from Soldat's back and shuffled to the basalt slab. Where they placed the bomb, carefully, upon the stone.

Lorak stared down at Zarak's corpse.

'It's okay, my love,' Quila said. She stroked his face. 'Is it okay?'

'Yes,' Lorak said. 'I've wanted to kill this man for seventy years, but now that he is dead, here at my feet, through no action of mine, I only remember the brother I once had.' He encircled Quila in his huge arms. 'But now I have you.' He looked up at the others. 'All of you.' He smiled at Anria. 'New family is better than some old bastard who stole my bloody toys anyway.'

Anria said, 'One of my brothers stole my underwear.'

Lorak chuckled. Quila giggled within his arms.

Laughter leapt between them, from one to the other, releasing the tension. Even Felice laughed, shared humour overcoming her grief.

'How long?' Lorak asked when the laughter died down to an occasional guffaw.

Haram flipped open the lid of the case to read the dial.

Quila hugged Felice. 'How did you find us?'

Felice brandished Medina's hair. 'Anria gave Medina a hair cut.'

'Is she dead?' Birsin asked.

Haram checked the detonator: twelve minutes and forty-three seconds, plenty of time to get outside the blast radius of the bomb.

'No,' Anria said.

'Good.' Birsin didn't sound as if he cared about her welfare. A new vendetta had started even as Lorak's lay dead on the floor beside the basalt slab.

A droplet of Medina's sweat, mixed with her blood, mixed with the essence of her, flicked off the end of the hair Felice waved above her head in triumph. It arced through the air, almost invisible. Haram saw it just as it reached the stasis sphere. He reached out with Shonri speed, but it was too late. He watched it land upon the surface of the sphere and held his breath. For a moment, nothing happened and then he saw the swirl of colour in the grey of the stasis field.

A swirl of colour that meant only one thing.

'Run!' Haram yelled.

CHAPTER TWENTY-FOUR

THE CITY OF LIGHTS BURNED.

Flames cascaded over the hills. Smouldering wood hissed as it fell into the slow-moving river meandering through the city.

Outside the high stone walls of the hill-top villas, within the walled gardens, jewellery, gold, the possessions of the rich, lay scattered alongside the soulless corpses of those claimed by the dead. Staring bodies, faces transfixed in hideous screams, of those who wouldn't leave their riches behind, of those who sought to enrich themselves in the chaos, and of those simply unfortunate enough to be captured by the dead.

In the shanty towns on other hills, amid the debris and the decay, bodies lay with the same horrible expressions, but most of these people had simply waited too long because their houses, their tattered slum-dwellings, were all that they owned. The poor always died defending what little they possessed.

The poor, the rich and every strata in between, died, mixed together on those hillsides, in the canyon streets between the hills, on the broad floodplain of the meandering river. Running, looting, screaming, they died. Forsaken by their protectors, their enslavers, the Magi.

A stream of refugees straggled out of the city into the broken world beyond, where they would fall prey to bandits and slavers, to the brutal life without the city gates, but here, within the city, the dead still lurked in the dark of the smoke.

Shop frontages shattered open, stinking of smoke and death. Taverns burned, houses burned, people screamed as they burned rather than fall prey to the angry dead—a terrible, screeching exhalation of a dying city.

The Pyramid, with its shattered panes of glass, with its diagonal walls blistered, broken, pockmarked by the furious vengeance of a rejected

Fire-mage, with its gardens trampled and destroyed by battles and flight, still shone light into the smoke.

In the chamber at the centre of the Pyramid, on an oblong basalt slab, within walls of glowering darkness, in a brassbound case, the stasis field surrounding the plasma of magic-destroying Shonri electrum fluctuated wildly. Flickering colours spun, twisted around its brightening surface like oil upon a whirlpool.

Eight Shonri, their Scryer-marks flaring gold, raced through the shattered corridors of the Pyramid. Skipping over puddles of still-molten stone, leaping through holes blasted in the walls, racing, running, heading always for the outer walls of the Pyramid.

The connection open between them, wide open, but even Medina couldn't push her way in to that tightly woven skein of consciousness. They were family, they were one, and they were running for their lives.

A hole blasted in the outer walls—with one thought they abandoned their race to the gate and threw themselves through this breach into the open air, skidding, sliding, racing down the perilous incline of the Pyramid with inhuman grace, inhuman dexterity, inhuman speed.

The stasis field flickered one last time and then failed completely. A ravening ball of superheated energy expanded into the chamber, filling it completely. Beams of energy blistered through the doorways to the corridors beyond, blazed through the walls of the Pyramid to the open air. Four beams of coruscation lashed across the city like the beams of a lamp, but blisteringly hot.

The Shonri ran on as the dead faded back into the ground to escape a pulse of light that outshone the sun on a cloudless summer day.

Haram realised with horror what the beams meant; that they must get as far away from the Pyramid as possible. It wouldn't contain this explosion. Something else was happening here.

The walls of the chamber held against the plasma. They sucked at it, tried to drain it, tried to contain it as they contained the energy of the basalt's matrix, the energy of millions of dead, but the plasma burned hot, so hot, so strong: designed, conceived to destroy magic, to create a dead zone where magic could not exist. It stuck to the walls, burned into their surface, through their surface, through the lines of force, freeing the basalt.

Through the dust, through the smoke, through the scattered, tattered, remnants of the city, the Shonri ran on. Pushing hard, running faster than even Shonri should run, their lungs tight, their thighs burning with the effort, their Scryer-marks blazing a golden trail through the gloom.

Anria guided them towards an obscure gate on the edge of the city. Her childhood home long since demolished and replaced with something grander, but the streets were still the streets of her childhood. The gate in the city wall closed, but Lorak smashed through it without breaking his stride.

The Shonri pushed on, up the hill, away from the city, heading for the small valley filled with trees where Anria fished for sticklebacks as a child.

Not far now.

The glowering walls failed. Their material disintegrated. The diametrically opposing force of their magic blasted into the ravening plasma of the electrum bomb: mutual annihilation, explosive power, heat, light, sound.

Haram threw himself over the brow of the hill, grabbed Felice, pulled her down. Lorak covered Quila with his massive form. Birsin, Soldat, Anria, Terin flung themselves flat, with only a low ridge of stone between them and the explosion.

The Pyramid crumpled inward for a moment, like a balloon deflating. Light glared from its cracked surface. It blazed from every break, every fissure.

Implosion, until the glowering energy freed from the walls touched the surface of the basalt. Resistance, as the basalt matrix cast off the ravening energy of the plasma. Explosion, as the walls of the Pyramid shattered and then vapourised in heat stronger than the sun.

Everything outlined in stark contrast, people's shadows burned into the rocks as the light burned away their bodies in an instant of flashing pain.

A moment only, then the rushing wall of sound, a blast-wave of air, rolled over the city, buildings, artefacts, drawing the ash of bodies into pugilistic poses, became a billowing wave front of dust, smoke and rubble.

The Shonri, their Scryer-marks shining so brightly that their whole bodies seemed dipped in gold, let the light blister the sky above them, let the wave roll over them, held their breath, closed their eyes, clung to the loam.

In the centre of the expanding wall of devastation, floating on a pool of molten lava, the basalt slab remained. It reversed its matrix, sucked all that energy, all that death, all that power, back into itself.

The light resisted the pull of the basalt for a brief second, but the pull was too strong. The wave front of dust rolled back across the landscape. The roaring wind silenced. The basalt sucked it all back and sank into the bubbling magma, untouched, complete, and filled with power beyond belief.

Silence.

And the dead wept in the shadows of the earth.

****

Night had fallen over the dead city. The eight Shonri stood on the hill-side. Their breath steamed from their mouths in the chill of a winter's night, but they drew their cloaks close around them and looked down upon the devastated landscape through the augmented vision gifted to them by their Scryer-marks; a pale, grey, monochrome image of broken rubble and fitful fires, not a hint of green in their sight. Every particle of life essence sucked away by the implosion of the Pyramid.

The dull glow of magma from the crater where the Pyramid had once stood. Steam billowing from river waters quenching that flow of heat. Very little left to show where the city had once stood. Broken remnants of walls. Some buildings, protected by the shadow of the hills, still standing. The lines of roads evident in the dust. Leading nowhere, marking only where people once lived.

On the hillsides around the city, the campfires of refugees blazing away into the night, holding back the cold, the dark.

'We destroyed a city today,' Felice said. 'How does that make us any different from the Magi?'

'I don't understand.' Haram's voice choked with guilt. 'The Pyramid should have contained the explosion.'

'We plan better in future,' Birsin said.

'They'll hate us now.' Quila pointed into the night, at the blazing fires of the homeless.

'With good reason.' Terin squatted on the ground, she couldn't look at the remains of the City.

Lorak placed his arm around Quila's shoulders. 'We did what we could.'

'We forgot what we are,' Soldat said.

'Which is?' Anria asked.

'Human.'

CHAPTER TWENTY-FIVE

H EAT SHIMMERED FROM THE SCRAGGY SURFACE
of the desert. Medina sauntered across the broken ground,
considering what she discovered out there in the heat. She
entered the cave, her hiding place while she sought answers to the
questions raised during the destruction of the City of Lights, questions
about magic more fierce than death itself.

In the cave, the magic flowed sluggishly through the cool rocks.

Such fun watching the city burn beneath her as she soared away. The
blazing explosion surprised her with its power, but the readings of her
pinwheels provided some of the answers. The Shonri must have carried
the bomb to the central chamber, expecting it to absorb most of the
blast. Well, the basalt had sucked all that energy into the earth with it
when it sank—a rewound detonation cascading such power as only
gods dreamed of into the realms of the dead. She doubted that Haram
had expected that result of his experiment.

The dead zone of the city. She laughed at the term because its double
meaning—a city of the dead that was dead to magic—would make any
further investigations difficult, but not impossible for a Witch.

She sighed and lifted the veil from her face. A shock of white running
through her dark hair, legacy of Anria's whirling shield. The dust fell
from the silk veil like ribbons.

Deep magic lay here in the cave, and out there in the heat, magic
that reached to the bowels of the Earth. The cave was a foul place to
live, but a strong place to hide and find what she sought.

Traders camped here on their epic journeys across the desert's dead
zones. She chuckled at the term again. Would she ever be able to hear
it without laughing? The desert filled with places where the magic of
the Magi didn't work; no Worm-train could navigate under its surface,
and no Manta-ship could fly across its sky.

The cave lay unused at the height of summer. No trade caravans braved such stifling heat, but the cistern, carved out of the rock at the entrance of the cave, still provided cool, pure water to quench the thirst, and the evaporation of the water provided a barrier to the heat outside.

Medina leaned forward to drink.

Something there? A flash of warning.

Too late.

Soldat's favoured weapon slipped over her head and tightened around her throat in a glimmer of folded-steel teeth. 'Where are the vials?' he hissed into her ear. His voice harsh, but beneath the cold restless touch of his soul burned the heat Medina always expected.

She wriggled her bottom against his crotch.

Soldat pulled his hands slightly apart; the teeth of the flexible saw bit into Medina's flesh. Blood trickled down her neck, across her shoulders, around the hard points of her nipples, slicking her belly, sliding between her thighs. The heat of Soldat's breath in her ear as he said, 'I'll open my hands before I open your legs.'

'You want this too,' Medina whispered.

The garrotte of steel tightened further. 'You took the memories of those I loved, took their deaths, took all that I held dear, and spat upon them, Witch. Do not presume to tell me what I want.'

Medina didn't answer; the tightness of the steel around her throat precluded even breath.

Soldat ever so slightly relaxed his hands. 'Where are the vials?'

'I'll keep them safe.'

'You'll use them against us again, Medina. I want them in my hand and then I will let you live.'

'Be gentle with me.' Medina said the words as a goad, but Soldat's reply terrified her.

He laughed.

Things had changed for him in that devastated city. He had rediscovered his humanity. She knew then that she couldn't play his guilt, his needs, against him. He had risen beyond that.

He had learned to hide his Scryer-marks.

Still Shonri, still a Mage-killer, still a hunter, an assassin of those that broke the world and enslaved all who survived, but he no longer denied his birthright. His indomitable spirit, the spirit that led him to raise the standard of rebellion half a century before, that indomitable spirit still survived, but mercy replaced his contempt for those left unchanged, for those who served the Magi still, for those poor people who only wanted to survive a little while longer.

He'd still fight, still kill. But beneath the rage, Soldat had rediscovered his compassion. No longer would he kill without a thought. The war continued, but the tactics had changed.

She slipped out of his mind, appalled at what she found, at what she had done.

'For this gift, I'll let you live, Medina, but only if you give me the vials.'

'You should kill me anyway.' Medina knew this to be true. In his place, she'd do nothing less. She'd kill him and burn his body, leaving nothing but ash blowing on the wind.

'I don't kill my own,' Soldat said.

Pain, such horrifying pain, surged through Medina's soul. It blistered her mind, drowned her in memory. She had been a child when Basilard found her. He had recognised her power and twisted it to his own ends. A Witch, born to the aether, became a Conduit, a connection between his Shonri warriors on the battlefields of the Mage Wars. She had revelled in the blood, in the death, in the misery. It had seeped into her. She wanted to be Shonri too, but the Machine refused her. It accepted her lover, Felice, but refused her, the pain of that rejection compounded when Felice threw their love away for her family, the Shonri, which Medina could never join.

All those memories without an ounce of conscience to bind them.

Medina sagged against Soldat's body. She wanted the steel teeth to cut into her throat, her blood to flow, her body to cool upon the ground, but Soldat removed the noose of the saw from her throat before it bit too deep.

'Where are the vials, Medina?' Soldat stood above her weeping body. The flexible saw already looped upon his belt, his hands on the scythes he used to cut and kill, his Scryer-marks gleaming silver in the darkness of the cave.

'I'm still me,' Medina wept. 'I'll not change.'

'You're a victim of the Magi. Just like us.'

Medina's tears dried in an instant. 'Victim.' She spat upon Soldat's feet. 'I enjoyed it. I was never a victim.'

'Yes, Medina, you were.' Soldat leaned back against the wall of the cave, but his easy stance didn't fool her for an instant. He could kill her in the span of time between the beats of her heart. 'You could've have been a Mage, Medina, but he took that from you and made you his plaything. Where are the vials?'

'I'm not Shonri, not family, not like you.' Medina stood, the cuts on her throat already healing, her eyes blazing once more. 'I'm a Witch.'

'As you wish,' Soldat said.

'The vials are in my strongbox. Over there.'

'I know. Open it.'

'You could have smashed it open, taken the vials and left this place.'

'That wouldn't have been a learning experience for you,' Soldat said.

'You bastard.'

'Correct. Open it, give me the vials, and I'll leave you in peace—with your plots to keep you warm at night.'

Medina considered attacking him; there were other things in that box alongside the vials. But he was Shonri, immune to most magics. And he was Soldat.

'I thought you sweet,' she said as she disabled the magical protections on the strongbox.

'You mistook guilt for kindness.' Soldat held out his hand.

She dropped the seven vials into his scarred palm. 'I collected Shonri juice before you even began your rebellion,' she taunted.

Soldat weighed the vials in his hand. 'Why?'

'Because I could.'

'You should plan better.'

'I didn't destroy a city… by accident.'

'You played your part.' Soldat closed his hand around the vials. The glass cracked, then shattered. Crow-black fluid seeped through his fingers, mixed with his blood, dripped to the floor.

He staggered and lurched back against the wall.

'Sympathetic magic.' Medina sneered. 'Connected to all of you.' She rose smoothly to her feet. 'Painful, isn't it?'

'Yes.'

Something in his tone made her look at Soldat's hand. He still ground the shards of glass into paste between his bloody fingers. His Scryer-marks flared brighter, stronger, from silver into gold. The crow-black fluid ignited, dripped fire from his fingers, every particle alight, and burned away into ash.

Soldat straightened his shoulders, looked down at the burns on his hand, and smiled a crooked smile. 'It was the only way to be sure you gave me the correct vials.'

The connection flowered once more between the Old Ones, the true Shonri; those marked not just by the Machine, but by their own desire to finish this war of the dark places and hidden powers, to destroy the Magi, whatever the cost. The connection brushed across Medina's consciousness like a soft wind: Soldat, Lorak, Quila, Haram, Anria, Terin, Birsin… and… Felice.

It faded away from her and she knew she'd never again feel its heat upon her soul.

Soldat wrapped a bandage around his damaged hand. Even Scryer-marks took time to heal such deep burns.

'Thank you, Medina.' He turned and walked to the mouth of the cave, then stopped and looked back. 'Most of us don't care whether you live or die, but Birsin hunts you now. If he finds you, he will kill you.'

'He can try.'

Another laugh. 'Goodbye Medina.'

He walked away into the heat of a desert summer.

****

The evening twilight fell across the desert before Medina ventured out of her sullied cave. She couldn't stay here now. Did she flee? She considered the question while she opened the strongbox and lifted the golden feather of a Raptor from within. Yes, she decided, this was flight.

She laughed, lifted the feather to her lips, kissed it softly, let the essence of those mighty birds slide within the edges of her soul and her mind, into her body, into her form.

Medina coughed and feathers floated out of her mouth. She screamed. Fell to her knees. The skin of her back tore open as bones grew jagged-edged into the night, as her muscles twisted, spun out along those new bones, as magic glimmered blood red in the darkness of the desert. Night fell so quickly here.

She cried out her agony, hands on the broken ground in front of her, as her wings grew. The last inching pain of telescoped misery as the golden feathers of a Raptor rippled outwards and ruffled softly in the breeze.

Soldat had rediscovered his humanity in the City of Lights.

Medina had rediscovered her true self, what Basilard had stolen from her so many decades ago. She was a Witch, probably the last of her kind, and sympathetic magic held more power than mere Magi could ever conceive.

Later, as she swooped through the thermals in the cool night air, riding the hotspots as the desert cooled below her, flying across the dead zones that would bring a Manta-ship crashing to the ground, Medina laughed for the joy of it all. Her hands gripped the strongbox, her body curled around her mirth; her wings beat harder, lifting her skywards.

'Never say goodbye, my dear, sweet Soldat.'

/ /

The Tales of the Shonri will continue in several stories to be published in 2014. Or you can go to http://talesoftheshonri.wordpress.com/ to read the online serial from which the published stories are culled, edited, and published.

Other Stories by Stephen Godden:
Kinless — http://stripminingmobius.wordpress.com/published-work/kinless-book-one-of-two/

Other books by Firedance Books at http://firedancebooks.com/
Fantastic stories: well written, properly edited, with great design.

Acknowledgments

MY BROTHERS MICHAEL AND CHRISTOPHER have heard me burble on about this publishing malarkey for decades. Mike pretty much read everything I've written (giving very cogent arguments about which bits are crap and why, as well as which bits are good). Chris once spoke the immortal line, "I'm not blowing sunshine up your arse," when I went all writerly humble about some story wot I wrote wot he liked. My oldest friend Paul always has my back on this stuff. So thanks geezers, here lies the first one.

Then there are the Writerlot [http://writerlot.net/] crew. A year and a half ago, Gary, Ren, and I invited a bunch of people whose writing we admired to join us in the Writerlot adventure. Some left and some joined, but we have never regretted the choices we made. Class acts the lot of them; check out their work on the site, you won't be disappointed. 'The Tales of the Shonri' started on Writerlot. This short novel is created from some of those stories rewritten and given a very strong copy edit. Without Writerlot it wouldn't exist, so thank you all. Here's to the next eighteen months and beyond.

Ah, now we come to Firedance. The collective, the glorious new experiment in publishing. On its feet and charging forward, devil take the hindmost and God look after all us sinners.

'ere look what we done built.

To my structural editors, Bill Webb and Patrick Le Clerc, my copy editors Louise Cole and Janet Allison Brown, my proofreaders (who shall remain anonymous, because no matter what *something will slip through;* pity the poor proofreader it's a thankless task, so thanks from my heart to yours), my cover illustrator Gary Bonn, and my book designer William Sauer. Thank you; any success this story has is a testament to your hard work and professionalism.

And to everybody else I have met along the way, those that helped, those that hindered, and those that shrugged. You all made me who I am, and in doing so made my writing what it is. There's a moral there. Don't pay the ferryman, kick him in the balls. No, that's not it. Don't look a gift horse in the mouth, the damn things bite. Nope. Oh yeah, don't put a preposition at the end of a sentence, use a parole board hearing instead.

Hope anybody who reads this work of fiction enjoys it. I enjoyed writing it, so there has to be a fair chance you'll enjoy reading it. Until the next time, yippee.

Stephen Godden

P.S. Ladies, Soldat is a cool geezer right enough, but Medina, she's da bomb.

About the Author

STEPHEN GODDEN writes speculative fiction. He reads pretty much anything. He uses the second to fuel the first. (And writes this stuff in the third, because somebody told him once that he should and he didn't like to argue.) Other than that, Steve's just a bloke of independent penury and incidental personality. He also writes under the name T F Grant. Well, gotta have some variety in your life.

You can connect with Stephen at the following places:

Website: http://stripminingmobius.wordpress.com/

Newsletter: http://eepurl.com/QZO2H

Twitter: https://twitter.com/PKgesic

Facebook: https://www.facebook.com/stephengodden.tfgrant

***Would you like the inside line on what is happening in my fictional worlds?* Join the newsletter and receive:**

Exclusive early access to: sample chapters, excerpts, short stories set in the same world, covers, and other content.

Free short stories in new settings.

Links to discounts and promotions before anyone else.

Access to advance reader copies in return for an honest review.

I have no interest in spamming your inbox. You'll only receive an email when I have something worthwhile to share.

Join the newsletter today: http://eepurl.com/QZO2H

Spreading the Word.

Thank you for reading this story. I hope you enjoyed reading it as much as I enjoyed writing it, and working with my editorial team to bring it up to the highest possible quality.

If you could spare a few minutes after reading this story, please consider leaving a review, however short. In the digital world we inhabit, word of mouth starts with reviews on the web. We live in a global community and what you say about the books you have read matters.

Writers write to be read, so thank you again.

Stephen Godden

Also Available!

Available from Firedance Books…

KINLESS: BOOK ONE OF TWO by Stephen Godden.
They broke his sword, they cast him out, and still he returns to fight
for them.

Rejected by his people, stripped of his honour, betrayed by the
woman he loves, Drustan desainCoid is naught but a sell-sword. But
when an army of demon worshippers attacks his homeland he will risk
all that he is, all that he holds dear, to deny them victory.

*Let the fight dictate the moves. Do not plan: act. Do not think: be. Let
the fight dictate the moves. Drustan opened his eyes and threw the spear
with a surge of practised muscle. He lifted his swords and leapt into the
clearing.*

Available from Firedance Books…

STILLNESS DANCING by Jae Erwin.
Lilliane has always been drawn by the desert — its emptiness, its eerie
beauty and its people. When she takes the trip of a lifetime to a Bedu
camp, she finds herself ensnared in a complex web of politics, blood
feuds, terrorism and ancient spirits.

Karim is trying to find his path in the material world and to marry
the girl of his dreams. But his soul cries out for the spiritual path of
his fathers.

Lilliane's and Karim's stories collide in a forgotten, blood-soaked
corner of Sinai. Brutalised, captive and bereft, they must find their
own ways to survive.

A taut, unusual thriller set in the fascinating world of the modern
Bedouin, *Stillness Dancing* shows us that the hardest paths can lead to
the deepest wells.

Also Available!

Available from Firedance Books...

EXPECT CIVILIAN CASUALTIES by Gary Bonn.
Jason has spent the last six years living wild on beaches. Now he's seventeen and a feral girl walks into his life.

A girl with no name.

He calls her Anna. She's fun, she's kind — and she's the most dangerous person in the world.

The most unusual love story, and a truly strange war story... Expect Civilian Casualties turns how we see the world upside down.

Available from Firedance Books...

THE EVIL AND THE FEAR by Gary Bonn.
An ancient magic released. A world of pain and fear hurtling towards catastrophe. A collision that will bring death and destruction to mankind.

Only two young women stand between the fury of the magic and the apathy of the world. Unfortunately one of them is dead and the other one is psychotic.

While her dead friend holds the fury of the magic at bay, Beatha must journey into the half-world to discover the secret at the heart of all things...

But a journey like this requires allies and, in Beatha's case, a truckload of medication. Is the world ready for heroes like these?

The Evil And The Fear is a wildly inspirational story about being more than people expect, and learning to expect more than you ever believed was possible.

Also Available!

Available from Firedance Books...

THE WALKER'S DAUGHTER by Janet Allison Brown.
When her mother dies at the hands of a silver-haired figure in black, six-year-old spirit-walker Cora Bloux hides out in her own body. Twenty years later she's still there, fiercely maintaining an outwardly stable, conventional life.

But when her own daughter is hit by a car, Cora is forced to spirit-walk again — and discovers that the spirit world has been waiting for her.

In the extraordinary, fast-paced world of spirit-walkers, body-swappers, rock bands and second chances, Cora must discover her true self and learn the ordinary lessons of courage, trust and love.

To see the world as it really is, sometimes you have to close your eyes and... walk.

Available from Firedance Books...

OUT OF NOWHERE by Patrick LeClerc.
An urban fantasy, pacy, funny and compelling to the last page...

Healer Sean Danet is immortal — a fact he has cloaked for centuries, behind army lines and now a paramedic's uniform. Having forgotten most of his distant past, he has finally found peace — and love.

But there are some things you cannot escape, however much distance you put behind you. When Sean heals the wrong man, he uncovers a lethal enemy who holds all the cards. And this time he can't run.

It's time to stand and fight, for himself, for his friends, for the woman he loves. It's time, finally, for Sean to face his past — and choose a future.

A story of love, of battle — and of facing your true self when there's nowhere left to hide.

Also Available!

Anthologies Available from Firedance Books…

THE FIREDANCE ANTHOLOGY – Words That Burn.
A searing selection of short stories from the circle of Firedance authors on the theme of "Firedance". A collection to paint pictures in your mind, tug on your heartstrings and whisper in your ear.

BROKEN WORLDS Volume One.
What do we do when God becomes an unwanted houseguest, you're in love with the wrong girl and aliens decide to eat California? Take a wild ride with 15 writers from around the globe to discover their version of a broken world… and the humour, compassion and love which saves us. From murder to manga, heartbreak to horror, *Broken Worlds* dances us through times, genres and worlds. Prepare to be thrilled, tickled, scared and enchanted… it's one hell of a ride.

THE BEST OF WRITERLOT Volume One.
Wild women, warriors, the first moments of love… Muses, metafiction and murder. Find new voices, new series and cracking stories in this dizzying collection from the WriterLot team. WriterLot.net produces great new fiction for its followers every day. This collection celebrates some of the best, filled with unforgettable characters, heart-stopping action, and the trembling uncertainty of personal relationships. It captures the essence of what it is to be human (or, in one case, what it is to be a dog).